COMBUSTIONS

THIS BOOK WAS PUBLISHED WITH THE SUPPORT
OF THE SERBIAN MINISTRY OF CULTURE AND INFORMATION

COMBUSTIONS

by Srđan Srdić

Original title: Sagorevanja

Translated from the Serbian by Nataša Srdić

This book was published with the support
of the Serbian Ministry of Culture and Information

First published by Književna radionica Rašić,
Belgrade, 2014

Book cover and interior layout
created by Max Mendor

ISBN: 978-1-912894-04-8

A catalogue record for this book
is available from the British Library.

SRĐAN SRDIC

COMBUSTIONS

GLAGOSLAV PUBLICATIONS

CONTENTS

ABOUT A CERTAIN DOOR
TO POST-YUGOSLAV LITERATURE

Srđan Srdić is one of the most important authors of post-Yugoslav literature. In fact, along with a few others, he is a writer whose primary interest is literature; he knows it and loves it, and is someone who, if he doesn't live off writing, which is hardly possible these days, lives for reading and writing. In today's world this is an achievement, especially when the logic of the literary market no longer exists, where everything is turned into wild plunder, in a futile rat race for a piece of glory and small amounts of cash. Srđan Srdić is a long way from this. He belongs to the authentic and important tradition which he chose for himself, which he gained with his own education and knowledge, and which he inclined towards with his writing: without paying too much attention to what is going on in the literary field around him. Although he did not appear out of thin air, one can claim that he entered literature in the most classic way, through magazines and literary competitions. It could be said that he rose like a comet and since his appearance things have not been the same in post-Yugoslav literature. This does not mean that everybody approves of him, on the contrary. But this relationship is changing, and it is not straightforward. In the beginning the critics were overwhelmed with him, but the readers were a bit appalled. Today, it seems that his readership is growing, but the critics are not as univocal as they used to be. The truth is that he does not care for either of them. He is treading the road he has paved, and with every new book he tries to cross new barriers and set new goals, to overcome the so-called "petrified form". Srdić does not do this because he is vain or shrewd, but because he takes himself and his job very seriously, and this is a rare thing around here, no matter what work you do.

I do not want to explore matters that are not connected to literature so I will try to go swiftly through every book Srdić has written – three novels, two collections of short stories, and a collection of essays. I would like to present to you the scale of his talent and his hard work, because we seem to forget that talent only constitutes ten per cent of success, work, order and scrutiny do the rest.

Srdić's first book, the novel *The Dead Field*, was published in 2010. It was kind of a precedent of the new Serbian literature, because it resembled the stream of consciousness and modernistic type of novel, similar to Joyce's *Ulysses*, not only by its free use of other generic structures, but also by its use of an experimental mode of language. The metaphor in the title instantly tells the reader what the book is about, but when one plunges oneself into the seemingly complicated jungle of the text and its meanings, it becomes obvious that the plot is set in what may be the worst year in modern day Serbian history; mad and inflicted with war, poverty and economic inflation, the year of 1993.

Like his great Irish role model, Srdić set his narrative over twenty-four hours of a terrible day, and just like in *Ulysses*, in Srdić's novel nothing much happens, or one could say that everything that happens is merely the overflow of the Lacanian Symbolic in the reality created by the novel. Two guys flee Belgrade because of the draft, while a girl flees Kikinda for Belgrade; their meeting, along with their deaths and love, occur in the middle of the story, in a village called Perlez. What is important is the story, and as a character called Srđan Srdić says: "Every story is significant".

Bakhtin determines the polyphony as the main feature of a novel. In his study about Dostoyevsky, Bakhtin states that polyphony characterizes the novel through different uses of language, by means of which it creates and resembles reality. In a similar way Srdić's use of various perspectives, his constant change of viewpoint, the rhythm of the narration, the style, enabling the characters to use different languages, and their significant silences, all contributes to the enormous richness and fullness of the text. The question of polyphony inevitably puts the question of the Other and Different in focus by giving the right type of speech to them without the slightest intervention. Through this approach, Srdić's novel becomes a study of character: a precise sociological analysis based on language and language behavior. Polyphony also brings to light intertextuality, which, in *The Dead Field*, is not only based on literary sources but also on music, popular culture and film.

Why is it important to write about the year of 1993 today, after seventeen years have elapsed? The simplest answer is that 1993 is key to understanding the dominant

Zeitgeist of today's Serbia. This shows us who we really are, and highlights, unfortunately, that we have not really changed since then. The coda in the last chapter is some kind of pessimistic conclusion to our lives. Srdić will blatantly tell us to our faces that everything has stayed the same. When looking at the past, his novel is an open fight against forgetfulness, against the illusion that we can negate what has happened and what is happening by turning our heads away, or sticking them in the sand.

Finally, Srdić's novel is the justification of the tragic sense of the world, which stretches from Homer to the present day. All of the characters are based upon this premise. Following the logic of hubris, which is reflected in the state of being different, the lovers, who are united by fierce passion, have to discover that they are related. There is the Angel of Destruction walking through Serbia: his name is Captain Zoran Cukić. Before him, even those who believe in the logic of blood and soil, and who are basically his kind, cannot be sustained. Only those close to the power will prevail, like Inspector Braca Josijević. In short, in a dramatic tour de force the reality confirms its brutality and spits in our faces.

Espirando is Srdić's second book, and his first collection of short stories. After the success of *The Dead Field*, Srđan Srdić was given the chance to present himself as a storyteller. And he did not disappoint us. He continued with his authorial voice, as he did in his breakthrough novel, and it seemed that in some of the short stories he went even further. Right from the start he shows us that he has mastered the form of the short story, which, unlike the novel, demands certain artisan skills, almost technical trickery; but in a few stories he did something that I consider to be the masterful touch – he managed to deconstruct the form, to reshuffle its pieces, and by doing so gained something completely new and different. He showed us that he mastered different modes of narration, that his intertextual scale is almost unprecedented in today's fiction, and that he can juggle the elements of humor and seriousness, and that, finally, he can, by the use of language, present authentic and profound emotions. If *The Dead Field* was an extraordinary experiment, the proof of authorial potential and bravery, then *Espirando* is the book that will bring Srdić to the highest peaks of Serbian and post-Yugoslav fiction. It is the testimony of the powerful and authentic narrative voice which (pardon my metaphor) can whisper and roar, scream and sing lullabies.

The architectural structure of the collection, which consists of nine stories, already tells us that the author knew exactly what he was doing. Not only do the stories have certain thematic similarities sketched into the titles, but they somehow melt into one another, which helps to create a loose novelistic structure. The common theme of all of the stories is death and its nearness; they represent the last breath, the moment in which the characters are still alive before the end. In other words, these stories are about the border between life and death; or are these stories focused on the thin line in between life and death: that exact libidinal experience.

In accordance with this theme, Srdić uses literary models which stem from high modernism. Although Thomas Mann and William Faulkner, whose story *A Rose for Emily* has been paraphrased or pastichized as an unveiled literary inspiration; still, one could claim that the true father of these stories is Samuel Beckett. The Irish author's breath could be felt behind every story, whether the story was written directly under his influence or not. Maybe Beckett's influence could be felt most in the building of the characters, which are similar to his Molloy, Vladimir and Estragon, or Malone. The characters are always in a sur-tragic conflict with the world. They have reached a state of disgust with life. In this sense, the way in which Srdić shows his masterful narration, and which brings him out of the generation is his use of strict and concentrated language, which is similar to poetry. By his use of language, Srdić manages to represent that exact state in which the characters found themselves, and which is very close to the inexpressible; such are the protagonists in the stories "Regarding the Death of the Best Among Us", "Medicine", and some of the characters in "Mosquitoes".

What is truly powerful is the picture of human consciousness in a hostile environment whose hate and envy are best felt through the impersonal "we", something which Srdić adopts from Faulkner. Perhaps "A Rose for Emily" is the core of *Espirando*, even though this story is further away from the atmosphere of the collection. Narrated from a non-typical perspective, this story gives us, as in an inverted mirror, insight into the inner life of all of the other characters in the collection. It convincingly describes the nature of the conflict that an individual can have with the world, even when he is a complete bastard, such as the characters from "Mosquitoes" or "Regarding the Death of the Best Among Us". Every time "I" gets into a conflict with "We", this conflict is fatal for the self, and this is the point in which we discover the tragic nature of the world, at least as it is seen through the eyes of Srdić's characters.

As in *The Dead Field*, where there was a chance for redemption which was lost in advance, in *Espirando* there are two stories which, regardless of the known closure, give us a glimpse of something different and better. "Medicine" and "Slow Divers" are extreme love stories, in terms of the emotions displayed and the extraordinary settings, but also through the portrayal of longing as well. One story is a romance between a guy and a dying girl, the other is a lesbian relationship with a flavor of antique bacchanals. It is clear through the narrative construct that both of these relationships are going to be fatal; but this intense tenderness which Srdić depicts is something that we don't see very often in modern post-Yugoslav fiction. In other words, no matter how short-lived these relationships were, no matter how much the fall from grace, which is inevitable, had been terrible and disastrous, the moments of bliss are the most important thing: they give meaning to life. Just like Bataille, by putting together Eros and Tanathos Srdić stands on the side of the former, because it represents the possibility of redemption from a gloomy everyday life.

The novel *Satori* was published in 2013. It begins with some quotes from Barthes, Lyotard and the Scottish band Mogwai. If nothing else, we (the reader) should be aware that we are in the post-world: post-structuralism, post-modern and post-rock. This is extremely important because the whole novel is set in a world that cannot be defined clearly: it does not belong to a unifying theoretical model. It can only be described as a world that comes after; it does not have a foundation, it does not have a basis on which you can build, it is a ruin which merely pops up. The protagonist exists and survives in such a world (or is he a postagonist?), who goes by the nickname the Driver. *Satori* is a Bildung, or educational novel, in which the reader follows the process of acquiring knowledge, revelation and satori, which in Zen-Buddhism means the moment of seeing the truth of the world, something which the Driver will not experience.

When the educational novel arose sometime in the seventeenth century, authors such as Grimelshausen, who is the father of the genre, or Goethe, whose novel *Wilhelm Meister* is considered the generic paradigm, had a completely different vision of human nature from Flaubert in *L'Education Sentimentale*, or Srdić in *Satori*. Every agent of education whom Wilhelm Meister meets along the way brings him some kind of enrichment of the spirit and expands his education. Unlike Goethe, Flaubert's Frederick Moreau regresses, i.e. his education does not flow in a logical sense from not knowing to knowing, but instead follows the protagonist's emotional development which is not balanced and teleological. Srdić's post-educational novel negates every kind of education which leads to knowing, because there is no world in which progress and/or regress would be possible. The world is a big ruin in every sense of the word, and the Driver and his friend Moki are like zombies, the living dead, shells that are bound to become part of the scenery. Their return to a place where they felt more alive than before, is as devoid of purpose as anything they had done before because nothing fulfils them. Meetings that occur along the way, which are not straightforward, follow the shortest line, but in a round way and are in fact goalless; these meetings will not enrich their knowledge, will not allow any insight or any satori, but merely serve to prove to the reader that the world does not exist, that it is completely ruined. Duma, the half-witted keeper of a farm which is also a mass grave; the Hun and his mother who live by the river and who will help the Driver cross it in their boat; nameless gas stations; the motel on the motorway; the officer who became a cleaner; the truck driver who takes the Driver to the wanted destination, and in the end Moki, whose name may stem from the verb "to mock" – all live in a senseless world, whose existence is completely irrelevant, insignificant.

Srdić does not escape the frame he set in his previous novel or in his collection of short stories. His closest literary cousin is still Beckett, but Srdić's theater of absurdity is enriched with a subtle ironic distance in the form of a key to understanding the novel. He is well aware which corpus texts he comes from, and at the end of the novel he extensively quotes from Flaubert's *Sentimental Education*. This quotation has a double function: it helps the reader to organize the text with hindsight, because sometimes the novel seems like a puzzle of narrative pieces and scenes, and this quote gives a certain teleology. On the other hand, the quotation refuses to be what it should be, according to the title – satori, revelation and epiphany. If the Driver and Moki spent their most valuable years when they were imprisoned; they weren't living, and the big question is whether such a life is worth living. The dark side of Srdić's poetics, which is set out in his earlier works, including those published in literary magazines, is enriched with the aforementioned ironic distance, which makes *Satori* his best ouvre.

Readers who love to play intertextual games, who love to explore soundtracks, who like self-quotations, will certainly enjoy this novel. It is based on a certain post-emotionality, on de-composure of every closure: from the narrative, to that of the created world, to those characters who are not able to dream one dream but dream two, ruin of the ruin. Nonetheless, *Satori* is a convincing mimetic picture of today's world, not only in Serbia, but much further afield. Also included in the novel is Srdić's political statement about the existence of PTSP, even against those who did not take part in the war directly. It is as if the narrative poses the question: "What is your world, what makes your life?" I am not sure that there is an answer to this question.

In 2014 Srdić published his second collection of short stories, *Combustions*. It comprises nine stories, which can be clustered into three groups of three. The first group, which provides immediate joy, are: "The Daydreaming Rat", "Good Night, Captain" and "Summertime". The second group, the one in which intertextual examination is dominant, includes the stories: "Golem", "Espirando" and "Leng Tch'e"; while the last group consists of the following: "The Leaden Carousel", "The Tale of How I.I. Settled the Quarrel with I.N." and the closing one, which in my opinion is simply marvelous is "About a Door". This division into reading classes should be taken with a pinch of salt, as a critical praxis which helps to ease the presentation of this narrative structure, and to show that Srdić does not give way to chance, because chance is the greatest enemy of art.

I have said enough about Srđan Srdić's masterful use of language. I could add that in these four books Srdić managed to tame the language and put it into the function of what he basically does with his writing; this is the description of *condition humaine,* which is not cheerful at all. Srdić goes even further in these stories, and the question that seems to interest him is the one of communication or, to be precise, the lack of it. This is where the title comes from, because his characters burn out in a fruitless attempt to communicate with one another, and with their surroundings. Whichever story from the collection you look at, you will see that the real communication is directed inward; there is also no significant Other. Even when real communication is present, as in "The Tale of How..." (which is a very gloomy paraphrase of Gogol's story), it is false, incomplete, one could say paradoxically unnecessary. If we raise this thematic level to an auto-poetical one, we realize that this is what literature does, it tries to communicate, but it often burns out in the attempt. It stays unread, or is either falsely or partially read. Its messages are like the famous Sartre's claim of singing in the desert (also quoted by Danilo Kiš).

Superficial readers could claim that Srdić did not move on from what he had already done in his previous books; instead, he entered a vicious circle of his own reading and writing obsessions. Nevertheless, in the story "About a Door", we can see clear signs of what will be the development of this still relatively young author. Not only intense emotional levels of the story which are visible during the mixture of narrative planes, skillfully jumping through the narrated time, crossing from third to first person narration, or the tone which is obviously more melancholic, even melodramatic, which could be compared to Bruno Schulz, but it seems that there is something else. The ironic distance of the previous text which had been extremely important, changed to auto-ironic because it brings about a further distortion of the perspective for the reader as well as the writer. All of this ends in a magnificent glorification of literature, marvelous auto-da-fe which enables life-in-art. If "Good Night, Captain" and "The Daydreaming Rat" depend on a completely false interpretation of reality by the characters, then the mild tone which the narrator takes, describing the kid/himself, presents a very important and valuable leap from negation to affirmation, from Beckett to Thomas Man, especially the Thomas Mann injection of irony and love. *Satori* ends with a long quotation from Flaubert, and *Combustions* ends with a sentimental tone in which there are traces of an almost classic beauty.

Srdić published another collection of essays, *Notes from Reading*, in the same year. Fellow critic and editor Ivan Radosavljević said that the book gives its readers insight into the master's atelier, as well as insight into the books that influenced his own work. Srdić believes that no literature was created ex nihilo, or with a simple touch of a muse. His deepest conviction is that literary artworks lean on one another and that they are born through the experience of reading. The nine essays deal with seemingly disparate subjects, from popular culture to Japanese literary modernism, but each essay shows us the depth of insight into the nature of the artistic world that Srdić has in the academic field, while also revealing the primary level of pure joy in the text. If his fictional books are sometimes gloomy and obsessive, then his dealings with other authors texts is in fact an opportunity for sheer *plaisir du texte*, as Barthes put it. This is why this book is a cheerful diary of his reading and thoughts about literature, while also being an excellent introduction to the books these texts deal with. His research is thorough, his texts meticulously studied and written in a very clear, approachable and understandable way, as one cannot think about literature in blurred metaphors, but through well-argued and clear sentences. Srdić's relationship with the literature shown in this book is distanced from the dominant theoretically non-defined blurriness which is more often than not just a mask for complete ignorance. For this reason, this book is in a way the key to understanding his fiction.

Finally, the novel *The Silver Mist Falls*, published in 2017, is the peak of his career so far. Radically different from anything he has done before, and from anything that could be read in the post-Yugoslav literary scene; this novel introduces an almost experimental prose which stems from the most radically modern and post-modern models. Although it should be read as a novel about the impossibility of communication, which is the closest encounter between two human beings, I would say that it is basically a love story or, if it is possible to say, it is an anti-love story. The book opens with a woman who is involved with a very complicated, self-absorbed and secluded man, who is also an author: this is probably the most testing love story Srdić has ever written. But the novel has much more to offer. It produces as many meanings as there are readers, and according to sale figures, the numbers are constantly growing. Which is kind of a surprise because one has to be patient to make it through this novel.

Readers have to accept that it is written in two voices and two perspectives, but they also have to understand a strange pagination, the sentences that begin and end in unusual places, to be in something paradoxical – the author is trying to communicate the impossibility of any communication – through language. If Derrida had written novels he would have loved to write this one. To make it easier for the reader, Srdić begins with an almost classic detective plot. But even if the person who Sonja has been looking for is found, the quest stays unrewarded.

The Silver Mist Falls has so much to offer to its readers – it is filled with almost everything that is important and terrifying in today's world: violence as its most banal emanation, the digital world in which we look for everything we cannot have in the real one, enjoyment in terror and horror, which are enabled through social networking and new media. Our scopophilia has peaked. However, the novel ends on a positive note, with some kind of dedication to the famous monologue of Molly Bloom from *Ulysses*. The world will endure, we cannot destroy it fully and someone will get out of this ill communication as a better person, as a lucky looser. In this sense, we could even talk about *The Silver Mist Falls* as the most optimistic of all of Srdić's novels.

Srđan Srdić is probably the most important author in post-Yugoslav literature. He is someone who shifts it from the inherent provinciality, whereby it was judged not only because it does not belong to the Grand Canon, but also because it is self-absorbed. The opportunity for the reader to read Srdić's stories in English is very important not only for the author, but also for spreading the word that in this part of the world there are authors who are definitely worth reading.

Vladimir Arsenić
Literary critic

No-one knows anything about anyone.

Fernando Vallejo

I'm not all men
I'm not all men
I'm just one man
I'm not that man.

Henry Rollins

GOOD NIGHT, CAPTAIN

Good morning, Captain.

Slint

There's somebody out there
Right outside the door
You can hear them breathing
You can hear them fucking

Gnaw

I'm a happy man and God loves me. It's fine in hospital, I've found the necessary time, the essential time. I do nothing in particular in this time, I only vaguely reminisce. Lelica comes then. We talk and pretend that there's nothing wrong at all. She holds my hand. Her hand is soft and wet. And nothing really happens and nothing will ever happen and I've been told I'll be an invalid after all, but this is not important, I know many that I have crippled and that we have crippled, I used to pity them, that was in the past, in the war (anything was possible then), now I know that justice is established, because, if there was no luck in their time, it's all the same, and what use would all the time and health of this world be to them if they were not God's elect as I am? I am happy and I'll be an invalid, Lelica will stand by my side, with a smile on her face, which is nothing but a signal of divine providence. Indeed, I might be awarded a decoration for something, the community could do as much. It would be nice to don the decoration and sit proudly in the wheelchair outside the building for important state holidays. Someone could give it some thought, and make a decision, an act, in accordance with the official regulations, a detailed analysis, which would on no account impinge on the country's combat readiness.[1]

I've met a man, we used to kill together. He asked me: *What's the matter, Captain?* I replied: *What sort of shit are you talking?* I passed him by and he stopped dead. I've learnt things in hospital and adopted many of them. I've learnt much about fools and unnecessary exposure to their influence. The army swarms with fools, you have to wait for the war to get rid of them. The war was good, but not efficient enough. No one will attend to my body and its deficiencies. I've got a good wife and that's enough. She knows what to do with my body. God is my witness, she knows.[2]

---

1   I stay in bed late since I've been alone. I stretch myself out naked, uncover and caress myself for a long time. The window is open, even though it's December. There's always too much smell in the room that isn't mine. I love my stomach. I've never given birth. That's because I love my stomach and the smoothness of the skin. I love to put my hand down. Then I don't think. I love not to think. There's nothing to think about.

2   I have short legs and it isn't fair. I have bow legs and I've suffered because of this. And I'm not tall. I've suffered because of this as well. Glasses, protruding teeth owing to which I hadn't smiled until I was fourteen... All in all, I've suffered greatly. That's because I've burdened myself with thinking. Utter bullshit.

The army is an armed force. A good wife is a force as well. What do I have after all? The uniform's fine. Epaulettes are fine. But, what concrete benefit do I have from them? A young fool from Tometino Polje confirmed to me that the Bible says so. There's nothing concrete for man. I must admit, uncomfortably, that I haven't read the Bible. I'm not given to reading, being a man of practice and action. Thoughts are an exception, and my head is so packed with them that it's a whole library. It's them I read. The young one was dismembered by a mine. I was watching, saying to myself that it was rightly written in the Bible, if he didn't lie. A little jerk, he wasn't buried with state honors. He wasn't buried at all. It's a shame, even for such a coyote as him, his mother howls somewhere.[3]

I feel slightly embarrassed when she comes. Probably because of the old men's pyjamas, but it was all so sudden, I grabbed the nearest things I laid my hands on. She tends to forget. I understand her, a tender soul. A woman. The pyjama bottoms are short, I don't know how, I keep trying to pull them down but to no avail. And everybody stinks terribly, there's no self-respect, people think they can stink if they no longer feel like living. There is a strange smell, here, in hospital. The army smells totally different. It isn't right to expose my wife to such things. It isn't her fault. She doesn't deserve this. Many people envy me. I've never lost sight of this.[4]

---

3   ... utter bullshit and a terrible fart...

4   The bed is large, I've always wanted one like that. I'm alone now, and I love to stretch all over it on all fours. Because I'm a cat. I put my head out and say loudly I'm a cat. I love to speak loudly and I love to listen to what I say loudly. I'm a cat.

I'm very cautious. It's professional deformation. I know only too well what many people think. I know well. But, I'm a commander of a constant guard. It doesn't take long before people start betraying your trust. No one is reliable. I've taken measures and I strictly stick to them. We have a wonderful, open relationship. We talk. We invest in the future of our marriage. Marriage is sacred. Mother is sacred. Fatherland is sacred. I promised her to do my best to make her a mother. She couldn't wait, she said, as any woman would. I'm sure she'll be a great mother. Like my mother. Great as the fatherland. I cling to this promise, this thought, one of those grand thoughts without which life would be a sheer load of crap. I swore to make her a mother, here, in the hospital room, kneeling down before her, kissing her hands, thinking she'd start crying, but I was wrong. She's a great woman. A woman-hero. She deserves much more than I'm capable of giving her.[5]

Ca-at. –at. I've got nice, expensive bed linen, I can feel it under my knees. Glossy crimson bedlinen. Despite the nicotine and tar-stuffed thin menthol cigarettes, there's still the youthful velvety quality in my voice. I can drawl well, I know when to stop. It's sexy. I laugh out loud and let out a velvety miaow. Freedom. I'm a cat. Catcatcat.

5   I've bought some fruit: apples, mandarins, bananas, kiwi, all I could find. It's all over the place, within your reach, in various baskets. I've done some decorating, I was patient, I care about the bedroom. I have breakfast: lying with my eyes closed and arms outstretched. I touch what I reach and pretend to be a surprised vain girl. I become immersed in it, sighing and eyeing the unexpected piece of fruit. I bite into it fiercely, its juice pouring down my chin and neck. I close my eyes.

There was talk in the news about a solar storm. I didn't get what it was. Then they showed the polar light in Norway. It's good in Norway. It looks so to me. I saw some houses in Norway, they seem to take care of construction quality there. You can conclude from this what kind of a country it is. I would go and see that. I can only imagine her surprise if I told her about Norway. She might think me a rigid man, not romantic enough. I saw it was snowing in Norway. That's romantic. She would wear a nice blue hat there, I would remove snowflakes from it. I don't know enough about this storm. What does the sun have to do with falling snow? They must be wrong. It must be a mistake. There's no sun in Norway.[6]

It's been reported that the storm can be dangerous. There's something radioactive there. I used to deal with radioactive stuff and I can say it isn't something to toy with. It's been said that people feel sleepy because of the storm. I've noticed it, everybody's dragging along like half-corpses, doctors, nurses, drivers. I'll tell her not to come over today because it's dangerous. And she might

---

6   Stockings are my fetish. I leaf through catalogues, ordering and trying on stockings in front of the mirror, posing. I want to have legs like those in catalogues. I cross my legs. I practise. I cross my legs and inhale cigarette smoke. The smell of menthol and good tobacco and fruit and the outside world. I think I'm happy. I've tried hard to be happy and the effort's been worthwhile. Each pair of stockings should only be worn once, which would be so exciting. To pull them on in a ritual fashion, slowly, like a royal, nylon cover, to stroll in them in town, to feel the nylon rub between the thighs. To come back, take them off, and burn them. One should have a fireplace. Fire should be swallowed. Plenty of fire.

be tired. It wouldn't be a bad idea for her to rest briefly. She might be sleepy. I know what I'm going to do, in any case. I know my own mind.[7]

I might remain bedridden or so, but I'd like to get married again. It would be better than the first time. I'm not satisfied with how it was the first time. I don't know if she begrudges me, but I would welcome a new opportunity. I'd bring over Ivan the Frenchman to sing the song of my life. No one can harm me, God helps me. And foes may hate me and wish me evil. I pray to God, I love you, sooty eye. I know she'd be surprised. And she'd burst into tears, that's for sure. The Frenchman is a gypsy, but it can't be helped.[8]

I'd give my life for those two eyes. I pray to God, I love you, my only joy...[9]

---

7   I first noticed it in the corner of the school yard, I was rising from the sandpit, we'd been practising the long jump. Fourteen years old, that was my age then. I was rising, on all fours. They used to laugh, but not then. I had small shorts on, smaller than I should've worn, I don't know how it had gone unnoticed by my mum. Who knows, she might've noticed, but she didn't want to… She's a smart woman. I look a lot like her. No one laughed, all the boys were standing behind me. A crucial discovery. A pure discovery. I stood still in that position for a while. How much power and strength in discovering who you are.

8   I still remember today the walls of the changing room in the school yard, the dark and the sound of the door being carefully opened. It smelt of magnesium, bad water and pubertal sweat. There was a parish house next to it, we had to take care, they could hear and see us. I still delight in this, in anxious anticipation, I have never changed. That's the most valuable thing.

9   Or the darkness in the basement, in front of the students' canteen and the day care room. Upstairs the celebration of the

Your eye captivated me, as soon as I set eyes on you. (Fuck his gypsy mother, it was exactly so, as if I'd written it.) I don't desire what isn't mine, I won't give my own, that's the way it is. I feel like breaking a bottle or something...[10]

Take off your clothes, I shouted. Take them off, you degenerate moron. It was around twenty degrees below zero and he was shivering and looking at me pleadingly, but I knew this wasn't the worst thing that could befall someone, there were some Russians who could do this, and there were others as well, but I couldn't remember then which ones they were. Take off your clothes, you moron. Those on duty stood silently, I lined them up at midnight sharp as usual, they didn't like my vision of discipline, but I didn't like them either. The moron started to undress. Faster, I bellowed, my command is final. Flabby and slouched as you are, what would you do, you sick wretch, I asked him, what did you think? Do you know who I am? Do you know who I am? Do you know who I am? He stayed in his underpants. I know, Mr. Captain. Who am I? You know nothing. I am the one who knows everything. Take off your pants. And I know who you are. You are sick, boy. Sick in the head. Lie down. The runway was frozen. Lie on the stomach, moron. Lie down.

New 1992 was in full swing, blasting with youthful music and firecrackers. The teacher of technical education, all of a sudden, a funny, balding man, what the hell are you two doing there, what's this, what the hell is this??? How sweetly we were moaning. Heeheeheehee…

10   Only arms and tongues. Millions of arms and tongues. Millions and millions.

Press-ups now, you depraved boar. Three hundred. Sing, your mother mustn't cry. You are insane. Your paunch is dragging on the ice, you idiot, you're going to catch a cold, which I don't want to happen, nor must your mother cry. Faster. The lieutenant stepped forward and timidly pleaded for the arsehole. He's punished, wouldn't this be too much, Mr. Captain. I kept silent. I didn't turn toward him. This country can't have too much of self-respect. Only self-respect matters. God wishes us to be upright and die as such. The boar must understand. Keep going, the number is falling. The lieutenant stepped back into line. Their wives aren't coming over. My wife has suffered. No one dares to venture. Cara mia, he called out to her. Several times. Upset, she ran up to my office. She told me about this scoundrel calling out things to an unprotected woman. He oughtn't to have done that. And then he fell. What's the number? Forty-one, Mr. Captain. Louder. Forty-one. Louder. Louder. Then I kicked him. He covered his head. I kept kicking him in the stomach, in the arse, I broke several of his fingers. I kept thinking of the creature's mother and it wasn't easy for me. However, I was sure that the lady wouldn't object to the execution of justice on earth.[11]

---

11   About the three guys: some of our guys we met in Budva in 1995, one was 27, another 33, and the third 38. I was with Jelena, and she was crazy, and nothing would've happened if it hadn't been for her. Hers was the youngest, his friends arrived two days later. They'd come to the seaside from Germany with plenty of money. Their hotel, on the first night (we only had one rented room), the car, the second night, the beach, the third. The car, the beach, I liked that, I'd never done it before. Three guys, never before. After that, I was a student back then, the three of them, we

You are a young man, Captain, but this has gone too far. He was sad. Not for me, but for everything, it seemed. If only you'd taken care. If you'd come sooner. I haven't had time, doctor. I fought in the war, and it ended ten years ago. And here I am, at last. The consulting room was sunlit and clean. You'll have to stay. I don't want to stay here, doctor. I have a wife at home. You'll have to lose a leg, Captain. I looked out of the window.[12]

Sometimes it happens that we can't fall asleep. You aren't asleep? I heard the biker from the bed next to the wall. At first I didn't want to respond. He's boring. Dying people think they won't be able to talk when they leave this world. I'm not asleep. I'm thinking. About

---

got out of the car outside my house, I was trying to calm them. In all possible ways. We'd been drinking a lot, before that. Spritzer. There'd been all kinds of things, before that. One of them was huge and fat, with a water polo cap on. They wanted to go inside. I was shrieking with laughter, trying to break free, the third one was different, younger, he wasn't comfortable, he knew nothing. I told them to shut up because my granddad was sleeping in the streetside room. They laughed like mad. I suggested going to the park, there, near the house, and that's what we did. We went to the park.

12   He couldn't do it. I noticed he was scared while we were climbing. He wanted to know where I'd got the key. You don't live here, he was surprised, but you have the key? I have everything. I leant against the roof terrace railings and spread my legs widely. I always did this in order to watch the town at night. He couldn't. He didn't know how to do it with me, because I wasn't just any girl. Do something. I knelt before the best guy in town, the owner of the best chick in town. I took off my glasses, on the roof terrace of the tallest building in town. The stars were above us.

what? About my wife. You've never told me about her. Who's she?[13]

It was the *Slava* and there was a din. We'd come together for the first time, my parents had gone out of their way, God rest their souls. She was unforgettable. Charming. It was obvious that she cared. She's always like that, wanting to make everyone happy. My mother beamed. It happened, she'd been waiting so long. You're young, that's what she said, she felt embarrassed and she stooped down. She gave us both a hug. The noise was getting louder and louder. I'm not good at dealing with it. I don't like elbows being pressed into my ribs while I'm sitting at the table, and forks, them I particularly don't like. People with flushed cheeks who keep too close to your face. Those who you see once a year and who take the opportunity to tell you all that you never wanted to know. I know my own mind. I need no one. Bad breath is another thing I can't stand. It makes me nervous. There was no toothpaste in the war. I can't bear incense. I felt itchy all over, I kept putting my fingers under the shirt. She'd gone, I didn't know where. Probably to the toilet. Or something like that. I felt itchy behind the ears, between the shoulder blades. I stood up. Commotion in front of me. It upset me. My stomach started to ache because of this all and I pressed it without anyone seeing. They were all looking at me, I knew that. I was their topic of conversation, with my young wife. Images kept slowing down

---

13   I once went and got a tattoo of a dolphin. It's on my back now, 15-20 centimeters, a tiny dolphin. I asked some of them what they thought of it. They can see it well most of the time. I don't know why I did this. I simply felt like doing it.

and fluttering, then dreadfully accelerating, fast forwarding. I nudged my way to the toilet, being approached by everyone, congratulated, tapped on the shoulder, I kept dodging and grinning as much as I could, thanking them. I don't know why, but I thought that the toilet door must be heavy, must be so heavy. Cabbage, corn bread, dried fish, all got stirred up in me. She was there, behind the heavy door. She was sitting on the toilet seat, with her stockings pulled down. You don't remember now, huh? Don't remember? Do you want me to remind you? You don't remember? I remember well, like an elephant, I'll remind you. I stopped breathing. Everything stopped. A bang, then. Teeth in the broken washbasin. He was crying out in pain, in a drunken voice, blood oozing out of his mouth. I held him tight by the neck and dragged him outside. Everything stopped. Fortunately, I always carry my service pistol in the coat. Nothing, not even rage. He was writhing on the living room floor. Cigarettes were burning out in the ashtrays. I pointed the gun at him. Only this, nothing more. To explain to them. I'm going to kill all of you. No one dared to venture. I can't bear incense the most, of all things. I'm going to shoot you all, each and every one of you. I could see her standing in the toilet door and pulling up her stockings. She didn't even shed a tear. A wicked woman. I tucked the gun back into the waistband. My mother came up to my brother, to lift him up.[14]

---

14   The solar storm? I don't know what that is. I know how to do a quiz in a magazine. I have a pile of magazines, they are packed with good texts about life and what it is like. I've read the letters several times, my dear, I'm Lelica and I've been on tablets

I've spent the day in anticipation and I've seen all sorts of things. I didn't see the solar storm, and it is said to be over.[15]

She hasn't rung. She must be too tired. She must be planning a surprise for me.[16]

I'll try to fall asleep. I'll be waiting tomorrow. I still have both legs. I still have a wife.[17]

---

since I was – years old, heeheeheehee. I've been married for a long time now, my husband and I have no children, heeheeheehee.

15   I answered honestly and got points. Do you practise anal sex, Are you bi-sexual?, Describe your most secret fantasy, Your best friend's got a boyfriend and you like him-what will you do?, Shorts: yes or no?, Are you in favor of having sex during pregnancy?, A twelve-year-old's dilemma-is it too early?, Your G-Spot?, Adultery myth, A gay's dream, Attention! A special supplement to the new issue-Nymphomania!!!

16   I heard a girl from a flat on our floor talking to a friend about me. She said I was super. They are nineteen, they look so. She's so... cunty, she said. I liked the word.

17   I'm going to leave when the night falls. It's more intensive then, more seductive, it seems to me I'm doing something forbidden so I have to hide, and I enjoy hiding games. Some day he'll come back, I'm ready for it, he's come back before. He'll be different, but I've prepared myself for it, I have a little calculation about this, heeheeheehee. There are so many, oh god, names and voices, arms and tongues, arms and tongues, millions and millions, like rats and cockroaches. I'm going to leave when the night falls, no one will have any doubts, I'm a serious woman, a highly educated woman, after all, I'm a married woman. I have my tasks and my obligations, day and night, heeheeheehee, day and night. I'm going to choose clothes, for a long time, I'm free, the majority owner of my own freedom at last, surely I don't like hospitals, they always remind me of something, something... What would I tell him, I don't know, it's going to be better?, it doesn't sound right, but he's so tranquil,

There's an old man. Near here. He simply won't die. He's slow and suffers from insomnia. Then he walks. He passes by our room, every night. He stops at the door which we never shut. He knows I'm awake and says *Good night, Captain.* Good night.[18]

---

so disciplined as long as he believes, he's a soldier and I love him because he's like that, it's going to be better?, I know nothing about it, I know nothing about worlds without music, smells, arms and tongues, I know nothing about the worlds of people with service pistols and nightmares, and I know nothing about the worlds with legless people. That must be it, hm, that must be exactly... so, must be so, but whether it is good or not, I don't even know the slightest bit about it. Why should I know? I am... a free woman, I can choose my clothes for hours on end, and step out naked into the street in the end, which I'm going to do sometime, but not yet, not yet yet yet. I hope he sleeps peacefully there, that man, what would he do if he didn't sleep, what would he think about when there's nothing to think about, perhaps about me, but that isn't what I would advise him to do, that isn't what I would heartily recommend. Perhaps I would advise him to do his best there, to find himself a woman, a nice little woman without a leg, or a breast, or something else, I think that place teems with such female creatures, and to show her things, because I've taken care of him and he knows that, I've done many things for him, I've shown him, I've given him a lot and he can't ignore it, if he has any honesty in himself. And afterward, when he returns, it'll be easy, people can easily agree, heeheeheehee, they easily split their freedom so they have two, or several freedoms they use when needed, he certainly won't be in the mood for abrupt and unnecessary movements, that's for sure. And me? And me? I know what I'm going to do, because there are so many things, things you can do, you can take in... into yourself... strongly... so many things... And that's why I have no qualms about this. I don't like dilemmas. I prefer to put my hand down. And not to think. Because there's nothing to think about. Nothing.

18   Sooo yes. Locked. I'm off. Good night, Captain.

THE DAYDREAMING RAT

Rats devour anything that can possibly be devoured. Man doesn't eat anything that rats wouldn't eat either. They aren't satisfied with this though, so even the dirtiest waste and excrement from human households as well as rotten carrions are a real treat to them. Unpleasant cases are also known to have happened, with rats biting even small living children.

Alfred Edmund Brehm

Rats can be carriers of human parasites, especially in large cities.

Wikipedia

Laki the kid thought of himself as one of sheer instinct: *No one is like me. Not even the mayor himself. Not even him.* That's what he thought. *No one.* He was greeted in front of the Town Hall. Some rushed up to him. A parade of grins at the sunny town square. Some staggered. Laki the kid, with his hand on the fly, the sun-drenched Town Hall façade. Laki the kid, with the same hand in the hands of condescending fellow citizens. Stumbling fellow citizens. *Our Laki.* Sluggish, and yet mobile, a bullet coated in fat. *Good afternoon, President. How's your family?* Hands in the pockets of an expensive coat. *You're all mine.* President of the Board for Gender Equality. Trousers pulled down. The hand again, stuck between the flabby thighs in the moments of idleness. The president. As he sits at the edge of an old hardwood table. A unique piece of art. The Party's commission, early seventies, last century. The president's melancholy look. Heels and stockings of fellow female citizens. The president's dreams as he masturbates in the office of the Board for Gender Equality. *You're all mine.* Sheer instinct. The phone. *I think it's your wife, President.* Secretary. That cow. *I'm in a meeting.* You cow. A glance at a young mother's cleavage from the top of the Town Hall building. You cow. A tissue on the too-sweaty neck. Thick neck. Wet tissue. At the nape. And between the legs. Four in the afternoon. A wonderful day for democracy. Institutions are at your disposal. *Goodbye, President.* Fuck off. *What if your wife rings?* Fuck off. *All of you.*

On the way to the hotel. I want to piss. There's no one there. Italian hunters, oil dealers, local piss-takers, all have left. A good, empty hotel. A good, empty town. *Good afternoon, President, done for today?* A meeting with overjoyed voters. Leave me alone. I want to piss. Suck it. They used to work well. A foundry in the plain, directors with a vision of a hotel on the square. A good hotel. A swimming pool, a sauna, a snack bar. I would piss into the pool. If it was functional. A good, dead hotel. I want to piss. A hotel in a state of dilapidation. Ghosts. Ghosts of self-rule. The president. Modern, profiled, contemporary. With a laptop in his hand. And some papers. Folders. Tiny eyes, drawn in the huge skull. A phone. Phones. In each pocket of the coat. Neat businesslike gait. *Hello! Good afternoon. Yes, please. No problem at all, it will be as I promised. The media have covered it. Our job is public, madam. We are under the magnifying glass of the public, madam. You know the worth of my word, madam. You think they would otherwise have been voting for me for twenty years, madam? You should know one thing, madam, this isn't the Wild West, and I'm not a sheriff, madam. All of us. The public's magnifying glass, we cannot hide from it. Gender equality. Everybody knows who I am. The public, madam. The public.*

In front of the hotel. The hotel in a fog. No one breaks the ice in town. Broken legs. Hips. Broken heads. A blue, metal board: the capital letter A. No one removes invalid boards in town. No one has time. Everybody has time. Abundance of time. The town of abundance. The hotel. Two hundred meters from the Town Hall. The president walks cautiously. He prevents any troubles potentially caused by falling.

The reception in the dark. Hazy silence. The electric installations produce a crackling noise. The hotel's night watchman. He is a daytime watchman, too. He lives there. He was told to stay as long as he wished. He could stay there with his family. Instead of a salary. The teacher. *Ivana, what's your address?* Humane character of the authorities. *The president has let you stay at the hotel? Nice of him to take care of you. You like it there?* Electric installations. Mainly burnt out. Mostly there's no heating.

The phones are out of order. The swimming pool is out of order. A decent hotel. For couples with small children. *No, teacher, we don't have a bathroom.* The pool is out of order. *You should be thankful, Ivana, for all that the president has done for you. The times are hard. People lead difficult lives. They have nothing to eat. Ask your dad.* The night watchman looks at the floor. *Good evening, President.* The hotel in a fog. Grimy windows of the hotel bar. The night watchman looks away. Thick, knitted socks. And beach flip-flops. *Warmed the suite?* A labyrinth of dimmed corridors. The hotel's night watchman, a bunch of keys. The president shuffles his swollen feet. The president pulls something out of the cleft between his buttocks.

The president's suite. Eight floor. Neon flash. Five workmen saw to it. They were told: don't tell a word to anyone. It lasted. About twenty days. It's fine now. Quiet, sentimental music. The heater. A light smell of paints and varnishes. Recently painted. Fresh bed linen. Stretched. A TV, a huge screen. A table, a comfortable chair next to it. *Ballantine's. Blended Scotch Whisky.* And a nice, elegant glass. Ice. A computer. *Wireless Internet.* Ultra-fast. A mirror in front of a double bed. You can smell something. Something like lavender. *You're free.* The night watchman leaving. He can use the hotel in its full capacity. *All inclusive.* The president has short legs. And a wife. And a little son. Short, stumpy legs. Bowlegs. And Italian shoes. The hunters brought them to him, when they were still coming. Now they don't know where. The hotel has breathed its last. The night watchman lives in it with his family. In the bowels of a corpse. It stinks, there. But, he doesn't complain. He's free. The president has told him so. And this is enough. One could not complain of freedom. The church is nearby. He's bought some candles. This is also enough. *Darkness inclusive.*

The president undresses. He touches a button on the computer, before that. *Microsoft* is humming. The president piles his clothes in a concentrated way. The president is humming. *The road to my farmstead is snowbound.* A denser and denser fog descends, outside. Utterly opaque. The president is naked. He takes his glass and moves the curtain. There's nothing. A tower in the fog. He turns toward the mirror and with the cold glass he rubs his gargantuan belly. An erection. Weak, but still an erection.

The TV, again. The huge screen and a weak erection. A brilliant set of channels. The president shoots for quality. *Silicone azure.* The president touches the huge screen with his weak erection. He leans it against the *silicone azure. The silicone azure* flashes by. The next scene: people at the table. The next scene: one is yelling, stuck in a heap of muck.

Illthroatfuckcreepyjewishfaces!

The president calmly concludes: *Always them. Nothing new.* High-quality program. High-voltage. The president likes the program. It's spontaneous and leisurely. Truth-like.

Fuckyourdeadchildinthegrave.

He likes the whiskey as well.

Tomorrowifyoudontmilkherillmilkyou! Andyouwon'tfo rgetthisaslongasyoulivedidyouhearmeyourottenbitch.

The icy glass under the testicles. Refined pleasures. The president rubs himself. Messages, one catching up with another on the bottom of the screen. The world is coded. *What did Nemanja do to the parrot? Skinny be strong. I just wanna say hi to Ljubica, Mara, Straja, Šile, and* *all crw from* Čibutkovica. *All married, divorced, older ladies sayhi to young, rich, handsome man sms*mms*042200200. ILOOOOVEEYOUUUU VIKI MY SWEETHEART !!!! HAK 4 all who know me... + i *. kissy kissy 4 lil pussy.. SHOW MY MESSAGE!!! management: we r sorry we don't have that song but u can send us another wish.. cernogod we'll play sinan, arshavin we don't allow swear words before 12 o'clock, Netopir there's a lot of messages so there's a halt, always with you the best audience your best management! Leave a comment plus+, and i wanna say hello to javi, dancan, nista, energija and everybody that knows me.* The president deconstructs.

The mobile phone. Extraordinary functions. The president knows how to choose. He tries to send a message every day. The matter of ritual. Always the same word. *Pussy.* All is said. They never show it. The president never gives up. *Pussy.* He feels good when he writes it. Sends it. He is sure that it gets somewhere. Things always get somewhere. He giggles. *Message sent. Pussy. Pussy. Pussy.*

The computer. An audio signal. A sweetish sound. The president puts his glass aside. He turns off the television. *The silicone azure* dies away. Someone has appeared. Slender, purplish letters. Kitsch. *Your chat.* A list of names on the right. A bunch of names. The president knows how to choose. *Apollo.* That's him. A name for a god. Like a magnet. The pimpled skin of the president's bottom and a pleasant touch of the armchair. *Hotty* calling *Apollo:*

hey baby
r u there
A slightly stronger erection.
aha
at the Safe Home

you
good
Fingers, thick fingers, clutching the glass again.
the best baby the best
hows the novel going
You stupid sow. What fucking novel.
having a hard time
too much stress
i sleep badly
too little
The president fights his way through the list. All women. All initial letters. Invite them all.
u have to take care love
 can i do anything for you
Invites:
hi how r u hi how r u hi how r u hi how r u
An erection, still.
aha
There are fewer of them than usual. You are never quite clear about this.
what would u like tell me
A few interesting gay *nicknames*. It can be good. Stinking fags.
what will u give me babe
u know i like everything.
no one can relax me like u
Replies are coming in.
Cutie: bok[19] *asl*
Ustasha.

---

19 A Croatian word meaning 'hi', 'hello'.

1985 m bg[20]
Another one.
student
u
Another one.
i got a firm
now im in vienna
 Another one.
footballer
im famous i cannot tell u my name straightaway
 Another one.
i never got married
no no i just wanted to be free
free forever
Another one.
built like a model tall gym regularly extra built
Another one. Another one. Another one.
my camera ain't working
tomorrow i'm taking a new one
my camera ain't working
tomorrow
camera
Another one. Another. Another. Another. My name's Stanislav. My name's Pavle. My name's Stefan. Sergej, Uroš, Andrija. My name. Mynamemynamemyname.

The phone. A blast in silence. Who's that, for fuck's sake. Aaa… (*The president has short legs. And a wife. And a little son.*) What a shithole. What on earth does she want now? Quarter to seven. The little sucker must need

---

20   Belgrade.

something. Tut-tut… I don't give. A shit. Shoo. *Hotty* says:

i'll eat u
cos u wasnt good
i'll eat u
cos u r a crocodocodile

The president closes his eyes. Images. Plastered on the inside of his eyelids. Idyllic painting. The charge, the sentiment. The father of a family, president, everywhere in the images. The family, obedient and meek. The little son, the spitting image of his father. The little love. And that woman. That animal. No idyll with that woman. With that stable whore. No idyll. With that fat one. That retarded fat one. She spoils everything. The president has so much life, so much life. Why sacrifice everything for her? His little son's mother. That woman is rubbish. Fat rubbish. A bag of rubbish. The president is there, in a safe place, and she will never find him. The president has found the solution. And he has his time. Time for himself. His four hours a day. The hotel, a winter afternoon. Five days a week. The weekend is for rest. God also celebrates. And why didn't she die in childbirth? *Hotty*, again:

and then i'll give you my bum
to do
all that stuff

He would be left with the little boy. A presidential fetus. An embryo. I'll make a man of you, son. You'll be like your daddy. And not like this. Pussy. Human fish. *Hotty*:

with that naughty tongue

The president doesn't see the words. His eyes are closed. The greatest of elations.

A fag invasion. *Kid95*. He sees that one for the first time. They keep coming. He's shown them what's what several times. Fag vermin. He's located one. There, from town. Unbelievable. Do they crawl there, too? He's arranged a meeting with him. A few months ago, warehouses, leaning against a railway track. Abandoned warehouses. A nice-smelling fall night. He'd brought a gear stick and a saw chain. He was slightly late. He didn't look like a pansy. At all. The president didn't look like himself, either. A mask of Bugs Bunny. I'll be the end of you. He whimpered like a sissy. Blood all over the dust and iron waste. You're gonna eat your shitty shit. He wiped his forehead. *YouknowwhoIam?* That's what he told him. *Lemmeseeyanow!* That's what he also told him. He lifted the heavy chain above his head. He thought of the town's coat of arms. A good conceptual solution. The president exterminates the sodomic vipers. All over the ribs. The knees. The back. He beat him until he broke everything on him. He unbuttoned himself and sat next to the piss-panted cunt writhing in clotted blood. He sighed. And voilà, it was good. *You don't know now, jerk. One day you'll be grateful to me. Your family, they're already grateful to me. I'm an exorcist. You'll all achieve gender equality. All of you. All, as many as there are. I'm telling you. And you know very well who I am.*

Kid95. A new whiskey for the president.

hey boy

how r u

Prints of short fingers on the misty glass. *Hotty*, a bit worried:

Baby

Boring slut.

hi apollo how old r u

Mechanically typed answers. Short fingers immersed in the keyboard blackness. A skilful artistic treatment of yet another possible identity. *The kid* is credulous. The president leads him on. *The kid* is a dancer. The president seduces him. The melody of typing. Letters, swift, across the whiteness of the screen. A miracle of creation. Inception. Birth. *The kid* is sixteen years old. An erection. The magic and symbolism of numbers. A virtual solution. Ninety-five. Those were the times. The president is melancholic. *The kid* is from a small place. He doesn't have a girlfriend. He's shy. He's a bit different. An erection. He's sometimes *here*. Most often at *this* time. He likes it here. He feels relaxed here. He loves to talk to older people. He feels relaxed with them. He likes *Apollo*. It sounds honest. Half past seven. Shower time. *Apollo*:

You'll wait for me two min

 Kid95:

i will

The bathtub, gleaming. A fine, intimate light. Dark red tiles. Barely visible ornamentation. The radio. A randomly picked station. The host: *Tonight we're going to hear a composition by Robert Schumann.* Barely audible Schumann. The elegance of a ritual in water. Showers are for yuppie-mongoloids. What kind of parents are those? *The time is out of joint.*) Who controls that little motherfucker? Control is the essence of the world. The discipline of mind and spirit. Self-repression. The president knows this very well. Seize a surplus from yourself. Strict control of energy. Things have their own aim. Who are those people with such kids? Control is religion. The president knows. This is how he's become what he is. It's dozens of thousands of hours with yourself. Rare are those capable of this. Chess patience is necessary. To position yourself. To combine. To reach right decisions. To have so many things in mind. To have reserves. There are so many policies. To align standpoints. Not to mislead yourself. The policy of ideas. The policy of instincts. The policy of family relations. The policy of power and its redistribution. The policy of politics.

A view from aside: the bathroom swallows the president's body. A powerful spout of water. The water stinks though. The pipes are too old. Sewerage. Sewerage is the problem. One should go down there. Dive down. Take a look. He's also heard of the town's underground passages. Who knows what sorts of things are down there? Who's prowling around? Condensation. The condensation of thoughts. That little pansy, what the hell… He should be fucked up. Brought to his senses. Shown this isn't a way to go. The president is almost blind without his glasses. The skin sizzles under the hot water. A meeting should be organized. A bulletin published. Conditions for a public debate should be ensured. On the following topics. Immorality. Perversity. Dangers that the scum of the earth expose the concepts of gender equality to. Puberty as a one-way street. The threat of juvenile homosexuality. The low blow of promiscuity to the soft belly of the traditional family. Proof should be published. The president has a tanker of proof. Correspondence. Photographs. Video recordings. Audio recordings. Internet addresses. Of all such. Resources for studying the problem should be supplied. To isolate the root of the problem. To observe it. To send the collected material to the media. To score. To profit. To occupy two thirds of the local newspaper front page with your own head. On a Friday. To cash in on the gained advantage. To acquaint the public with the scope of the endeavor. To profit. *Profit. Profit.* There was a case of a deaf-mute woman. Abuse. Father raped his stepdaughter. The town teems with good examples. To gather them all. To take photos with them all. To promise them all. To embrace them, in a fatherly fashion. In the name of the concept. To bow down to gender equality. Emptying of the testicles across the dark red tiles. *Here you are, Hotty, hereyouarehereyouarehereyouare.*

The president wipes himself. A silky, warm towel. Quarter to eight. A perfect timing. A suit, a tie. Glasses. A cigarette. A real one, imported. From distant islands. Preparations for the master ending. Well, I gotcha, you little pansy. *Kid95:*

apollo i have a song for you
when you r back

Disco balls. The aged fag twerks. A half-breed and a drummer with an idiotic mustache. An invisible saxophone. Gross. Gross, gross... *Hotty:*

jerking off baby

The keyboards are irritating. Getting on nerves. The president wants to leave. To go out. Into the fog. His world has been contaminated. It's been occupied by fags. His four hours with himself. With rustling female *nicknames.* Someone has to pay for that. *If you want my body and you think I'm sexy come on sugar let me know.* Fuck you. All of you. *Hotty:*

come on baby

I have a wife, you pansies. I have a son. Get off my back. *If you really need me just reach out and touch me come on honey tell me so.* The president, with his phone in one hand. A good camera. One of the best.

i d love to see you kid

got a camera .

The president knows what a cutter's job is. *Kid95:*

yes

like the song

I'm going to record you, cunt, just come. You'll become a star. I'll hang you. In the sky of the Net. *A secondary school student shows his ass.* You'll be fucked by everybody after that. You'll withdraw from all the schools of this world. You'll move out of all the towns and villages. You'll go mad.

aha...

you turned me on

got a camera

Neighbors, homeroom teacher, mummy, daddy. *Kid95:*

Here

Ringing. The phone. Her again. The president's rage. The president rises. Turns his back to the screen. Answers. The fat woman's voice. The tired fat woman. *What do you want?!!! What do you want?!!!* A pause. Water. The faucet in the bathroom isn't fully turned off. Drip. Drip. *What do you want?!!! I'm working, they've been fucking me all day long, who can explain to you what gender equality is?* Drip. *Who is sick?* Drip. Drip. Drip. Drip. *What the fuck is the matter with him?* Dripdripdripdripdripdripdripdrip. *Why is he sick?* Tons of fog all over the window panes. Silence. Only the water. And the fog. A good, quiet town. *It's you who are sick, damn you. You're both sick. You and he.* Drip. *Here I come to cure you, sick mothers' moron sons.*

The best camera, no doubt. The president turns around. He thinks about the dignity of the finals. He daydreams, which lasts for less than a second. The screen. The boy. A sixteen-year-old in a darkened room. A thermometer on a messy pile of clothes. A dumb expression on his face. Bewildered. As if he's chewing. Ungainly, fat rolls all over his body. A hand in between his pinkish thighs. Naked. Like a baby. Completely naked. A little son, the spitting image of his father.

Hotty:
coming baby
ah ah ahhhhhhhhhhhhhhhhhhhhhhhhh...

Midnight. Church bells. Laki the kid on the square, just moved away from the hotel. He doesn't know where. All directions buried under the fog. Dead silence. Laki the kid stands still. A heavy provincial dream in the fog.

THE LEADEN CAROUSEL

This one's called Iron Horse, born to lose.

Lemmy

They talked – I believed, about a shot into the night light, buckshot that instantly untangled some wires on power lines, about sparkling confetti of the blaze and traces of gunpowder among burgeoning sparrow-size snowflakes. This is what I found in the witnesses' words, ready both to lie and to retract what they said, for the sake of nicer tales about him, who has always been from tales, about whom one could always say anything, which is as true as anything else. They said he'd been standing there for long, in the street of a national hero whose grandson managed an inn where people stopped by on their way from the railway station, they didn't say, but I know he had two pairs of woolen socks (an old woman always gave them to him, cooing and saying how he had nobody and how she herself, old as she was, would be better than nobody for him, so he could call her both grandma and mother), which warmed him under his unlaced safety boots. And I know, though nobody uttered a word about it to me, how he clutched his sporting rifle, but I also know, and there's no evidence, that what he rolled and chewed below his heavy, tobacco-reeking mustache was equally pungent and raw, as he was himself, furious under the moon-light. All kinds of scoundrels, pudgy from pigs' tails and curdled, overdone blood, milled around the nooks and winding paths soiled with sludgy snow, disheveled slov-ens with wet legs howled, emboldened by the New Year's Eve craze, pissing all over solitary transformers scribbled over with their children's names, turning around (as such brethren turn around all their lives, timidly expecting a knife in the small of their backs), belching and blow-ing their large noses under the frozen windows. Voices from the television, throaty singers, cheap Chinese pyro-technics, rubble of slivers and protruding jaws, whistle of the last December wind through the skeleton of the God-forsaken church of forsaken Germans, cracks on the unstitched walls, witches burrowing as they bathed in the muddy underground waters. And no-one dared to approach him, although they would never admit this, no-one dared to approach him, because they knew what came out of his thinking in silence, when he devoted himself to the idea of his gleaming gun, stolen and resold three times to bandits who expressed an interest in them. He stood there, like the formidable Genghis Khan, with his gun and a clenched fist, preventing the plaintive Calendar from approaching us, he lamented, wailing over the mediocrity of all offered places, times, men and women. This I know, what he thought, as the audience dispersed in the dark, motionless, rooted to the spot, implacable, he went on about detonations, hur-ricanes of burning gas in which everything disappeared and which cleaned, cleaned, cleaned. No-one knows how he knew that there, in the snow-sprinkled thick-et, was Kuburić, bedraggled and squatting, who owed to him, as many did, as all did, as he thought of them all. Nobody was present, but everybody knows, that he called this Kuburić guy and told him: Come 'ere, you animal, chewing on the cut end of a nervously rolled cigarette, showed him the shot-through wires swaying in the air, like a newly blossomed but already dried flower, motioned for him to climb the slippery pole and to tie, Tie!, he yelled at him, and the man started to run home after all, all the while stumbling and collapsing along the snow-bound table of the road, Tie!, he howled, thinking of knots, inextricable, I know this was so, no-one has to tell me, about knots tied by thousands of silly sailors simpering and loudly singing what couldn't and mustn't be imagined. Come 'ere, lemme tell ya!, he barked, alone on the road, in a greasy fur coat, when the clock on the Orthodox church struck midnight, and poor fireworks surged into the pregnant sky. And no-one was there to hear the man with a gun, Happy New Year and all the best, there, behind the thick walls, Nobody wished his Son all the best, who in turn congratulated his Mother on giving birth to him, all heavily laden with hope, wishes and oversalted roast meat. Lemme tell ya!, he grunted, Moloch's shadow above the disguised village, and feeble, grimy Zo saw it, he sees everything, an eternal village traveler, a solitary village walker, because he passes and watches, and takes what he's seen who knows where, and doesn't tell it to anyone as no-one asks him, who is nobody's, to the village's shame, and everybody's, also to the village's shame. Zo the dumb animal saw the cooled barrel turning again toward the freshly bound electrical wound, but what could he do, and what could anyone do, you can do nothing to the dark and that's it, and who doesn't know this knows nothing and then it's all the same this way or that. The dark greased the road, and Zo didn't get frightened, since he'd also come from the dark, the dark was good for him and that's where they'd like to leave him and his mother, untidy and disheveled and locked in a yellow shanty on the Tisa, but I'll have to say a few words about this, and this, and this. And Zo heard, which I know very well, that one commanding: Lemme tell ya who I am, stand still there! I'm On, I'm Off! On!!! Off!!! On!!! Off!!!, that's what I've been told happened that night when a murky snake-like year dragged itself nonetheless, misplaced in the utter provincial gloom, howling under duvets warmed by carcasses, retreating behind wooden coal boxes and darting its tongue at the holiday spew. This is how it was that night, when a man with a gun decided to kill the night sun twice.

And I suppose that Zo was also present when the thing with Tešić's pigs and dogs occurred, as he was the only one who didn't mind that muddle-headed sniveler who followed him at a good distance, not wanting to check himself what it could have been, and he was the only one who didn't mind when it had already taken place, and when the poisoned cattle started to writhe in pain in Tešić's yard, all of a sudden, as if the curse had arrived from nowhere. Out of four Tešić's half-wild dogs, which prevented even his family from getting hold of the gate, only one sadly looked around, putting out his front right paw toward something, not knowing himself toward what, the poor thing, because he was all of an animal reflex while the others were dying in horrible spasms. This slobbering Zo came into Tešić's yard, now unprotected by irate curs, shoved his way through the crowd, which was composed of all sorts of people, from old Tubić to that fat Paja, who was always saying he'd never eaten so much that he couldn't eat another roast chicken. As the vet bent over an overturned sow, Zo was passing by, eyeing now the guinea fowls, now the ram, going around the whole of Tešić's mess, mute, helpless and abandoned, and then the vet uttered the word poison, at which all of them shuddered and looked toward the other side of the garden, where, behind the weeded plot, stood that house. Zo could step into that house whenever he wished, and he wouldn't say anything to Zo, perhaps: Here, scarf it down!, and he would throw him a slice of fried meat to gnaw at and strengthen the few teeth left in his mouth, since doctor Neno also said it was no use bringing him (when an idle woman caught and took him to the health center), as that's the way it is and he's as such and he'll croak as such, maybe now, at fifteen, maybe at a hundred and fifteen, because it's just that sort of a badger that you cannot make head nor tail of it, let them leave him alone to loaf wherever he wants, and he's got a mother too, she could strangle him if she doesn't like the way he is, how and with whom she gave birth to him, let her strangle him now the same way. And Tešić's children, whom he has three, all started to whisper among each other, burly as bears and lazy as their father had always been, so they began to threaten the merry poisoner that was now laughing and enjoying himself after the slaughter, because it was him, it could be nobody else, as it was also him who shot into the wires for New Year's Eve, and Tešić had long been saying that the end of the world would be when all those who arrived after that war joined with all these arriving after this war, then it would occur to those who didn't believe him when he told them how he'd seen with his own eyes their three hundred Bosnian swines, he'd seen their invasion on some respectable people's land and he'd seen the devastation left behind, worse than that caused by locusts. However, Tešić and his father Milenko had prepared for evil a long time ago, equipping themselves with arms and waiting, and now a blow came their way too, by their next-door neighbors this side of the road, deliberately, for no reason at all, because Tešić can say what others can't, about who comes, when they come, who leaves, when they leave, what the talk is about, about the trucks with no license plates stopping in front of his house, about weapons, about the guy who owns a kiosk in the center and all the pigs Evening Newspapers reported on (there was also an interview with some villagers, where it was stated that Tešić said: Stop the pigs' oppression!, and Tešić did say something, but not this, he said something totally different, which was pure truth and nothing else, and he hoped they would read this, both he and all his pals, so they would be at least a little ashamed of what they did to people safe and sound and their fields). Let Triglav speak up too, since he can also testify that he almost lost his head when that one came to the leprous loafer's mother, whose father no-one had ever met, to mow the grass in front of her house, and he sat on a little bench that had been placed by the late granddad Vico, and they say it was Lujza in her time, and there he was sitting, musing over something when Triglav got out to feed the cattle. As Triglav was calling to his wife from somewhere, the one on the bench suddenly stirred, and next to him was the little scarecrow Zo, possibly to groom him like a nag, and Tešić was told to ask the mute boy if he would scare Triglav a bit, he nodded his head, having already drawn his big gun, and started to shout: Ma-hae!, as he always does when the devil has hold over him, Triglav turned around, but it was late, a bullet had already buzzed above his head and dug itself into the summer kitchen wall, I surrender, stop the fire!, yelled Triglav, not because he is a coward, but because a man cannot cope with the crazy bird-brained blockhead. The little one was all the while hopping, now on one, now on the other leg, hugging and kissing him, as if wanting to say something, but not being able to since he was born not to be able to do what he wants, and to have to do what's left for him to do, what no-one else wants. Triglav doesn't have to either if he doesn't dare, he, Tešić, will send the carcasses to Novi Sad to be analyzed, his daughter is a student and she knows people, and he will go straight away to the local board of the Serbian Renewal Movement, let's see what they'll have to say there about everything, now that the old with the new Bosnians have started to poison their members and founders. As soon as he heard his own name, Zo sneaked away, I'm sure it was so, because he didn't like being called, since whenever he was called, it wasn't any good, and he became sorrowful at the mention of these two letters, so he reckoned he'd better go alone than being assaulted by them, he'd better go all the way round into the next road and the yard on the other side, where that one is motionless and silent, to see whether he can give a hand, although Zo himself, such as he was, realized that there was no help there whatsoever.

It hadn't been long since the extermination of Tešić's cattle when I set off to see and hear him myself, and even if he didn't say anything, to be there, to sit a while, because there are things that man does but there's nothing behind them, no background, and these are things rare and precious, and it's then that man is the most at being man, thus I went past the Castle, then by the house in which those people were suffocated by gas, and I recalled quite clearly how granddad took me to that house to see the suffocated people, later on he also got suffocated, but in his sleep, him I didn't see, something happened, as it happens to the photos in which a man stands next to some people dear to him, and then it's all gone and he doesn't know who they are and how he ended up with them, and he even hates some of them, when the time comes for hatred. I couldn't simply get in, so I shouted: Hey there!, and then nothing, so I shouted even more loudly: Hey there!, at which he asked who I was and I said it was me and he told me to be free to get in and that there was nothing to be afraid of. As soon as I got in, I found him sitting on the porch, in front of him a wooden, cracked table with bread, garlic, meat and salt, a knife, soup with chicken necks, all steaming, donuts that who knows which woman had made and brought him, as there were women who came here whose husbands pretended not to know about this, sometimes it's smarter this way, because a man who wants to know everything eventually has nothing to do with his life except either to go mad or to go down into a deep well never to get out of it until the day when each one will have to confess what's been done. How's it going?, I asked him, and he looked at me with those bright eyes of his, the way old dogs look, calmly and benignly, as it would seem to anyone, but you don't know, you don't know what there is, I'm eatin' meatee, and he pushed the greasy plate toward me, so that I too could help myself, and it was so enjoyable outdoors, not a voice was heard, insects and birds, as if they owned the world and could get away with anything, over those weeds of his, he'd never cultivated his garden, he mocked his dead parents by doing not a single thing they'd told him to do. Then there came someone else, the very voice vibrating in front of the house, calling out humbly and beggarly, and we were sitting and I couldn't breathe, a bite was stuck in my throat and in my hand there was a slice of bad white bread which crumbled and disintegrated under the fingers, Who's that one?, he told me and I didn't know how I could possibly know, then Who's he?, and he glanced at the stick on which a rear-view mirror was hooked, so that he could see who was in front of his house and who was getting in, while his presence couldn't even be anticipated by anyone as he sat on the porch. Babuš, I said, and he stopped, then moved backward and leant on his chair, thinking a little, and then he told me quietly: That one can't come in, and I agreed to this and we kept on eating as if nothing had ever happened, and the Gypsy whined a bit longer, until he was gone as anything in the world might be gone, as well as the world itself. As soon as the sun approached the earth, there also came a truck, we hadn't spoken much before that, I can't even recall if we'd told anything to each other, it's often so, there's nothing one can say, so it's better not to force it, we must have fallen asleep for a while, stuffed as we were, when we were roused by a horn, I took a look at the rear-view mirror and said: A truck, and he retorted he could hear it himself, and I replied that he could hear it, but I could see it, some man jumped out of a huge trailer, that one went straight into the yard without asking a thing, and took the right of the two concrete paths in between which dandelions flourished. That one dragged himself along, without being offered at all, except the question: What's up today?, at which, all lop-sided and blind, he answers: Come and see, he motioned for me too to come along, and the blind one got mad: Where's he going?, and he replied: Who are you to ask me?, and he cast him such a look that any other word got stuck in the blind one's throat, and he didn't even think of pulling another one out of there. The driver got out too, saying he was from Bijeljina, half beans, half wall panels, that was what he got that day, he blinked in my direction, then he snorted like a pig and shouted: Huhhh?, and I approved, whatever there was to be approved of, and two more started to unload, now already in the dark and to the sound of crickets, taking everything into the house, into the cramped room where his granddad had been dying for years. We were rolling our cigarettes while they were working, he was silent, but then he suddenly said: Last time it was dolls and asbestos clothes, I didn't reply, he fell silent again, then he burst out laughing so strongly and heartily that tears started to run down his face, Imagine those robbers and dealers, dolls and asbestos clothes, what on earth can I do with them, you brainless shit-eaters and sons of whore mothers, and he kept on laughing as if there had never been anything funnier nor would there ever be. We drank now beer, now rakia, and I was starting to feel woozy when they finished unloading, and he told them to close the gate behind them, so we rose, he ordered me to follow him, I got into the house after him, he bent down and fetched an automatic rifle from under the bed, because these were lying all around, these were being brought and I knew that, and you'd better not know what you know, he stood on the dining room doorstep, tilted the rifle and riddled the ceiling with bullets, mortar was falling down all over the room, dust was gushing from all sides, and I told him nothing, nor did I know anything about what he was doing, he clenched his teeth and whispered: Clear off, you too, as long as your head is on your shoulders. Somewhere along the road I met the crazy woman in rags and her mute son, I asked her where she was headed for, the unfortunate wretch, at this hour, and she told me she was going to tidy his place up a bit, dragging that kid along, who was kicking and trying to get away, she must have roused him from his sleep and made him come along with her, such as these are afraid of the dark and anything one could be afraid of, more than any of god's common creatures.

There were many at Švraka's inn that night, it's a village and everybody comes, father, son and grandson, and what's even worse, daughters also crawl around, putting straws into beer bottles and then hiding somewhere behind, as if there was no-one behind, as if nothing could be seen nor heard, as if anything could be hidden at all. There was a musician from Zrenjanin, a man-orchestra in a gray jacket which the firm had provided him with in order for him not to appear at anniversaries and celebrations looking like a scrag, he had a guitar and a small amplifier, and he was yelling that Keka's got young girls who do anything for money, hardly anybody was listening, some of them were looking in the direction of a Slovenian television, two channels, the first or the second, most often the first, as soon as he saw it, the musician got angry and he blew into his gourd, and this was his show and the instrument only he could play. Once I left the town, I thought it was all concrete over there, many wetted themselves, Švraka didn›t take care of the toilets, there was a queue, who couldn't wait had no choice, It's so difficult to endure, that song was being on, those in the front rows were making faces, Let there be light, let there be the sky, let there be the earth, Zo was also there, he didn't bother anyone and nobody noticed him, there were some with foreign currency bills, those were the same people with pigs, kiosks, bombs and similar articles, the crowd was unbearable, but I had nowhere to go, and it was too hot and mosquitoes flew over from the Tisa, and anyway nobody was waiting for me at home, this is my choice, that nobody waits for me at home, nobody and never, this is the easiest way. Zo was sucking juice from a glass bottle, getting all sticky, a new song began, What's that over there we're all running away from?, no-one was paying attention any more, the inn was swollen with the odor of the bodies, when he burst in out of the blue, the local bullies made way, since they know very well what goes into what, the sound of the gourd anew, he came up to Zo and hugged him, no-one was surprised, such things happened that this was a trifle, and when Švraka jumped dead drunk into the small pool he'd built in his garden, which lasted for a couple of days and no-one mentioned it any more, this is how it is when there's too much of everything, then there's nothing for the future. He was kissing Zo, who was trying to break free, I could clearly see, I wasn't far away, I tend to withdraw and stand aloof, in order to be able to contemplate from a distance, and Zo wasn't dodging because the touch of his lips was unpleasant, but because he wasn't used to being kissed, he didn't understand why people did this, he'd never been told and explained. Then he took him by the hair and looked him in the eyes: Speak!, but in fifteen years Zo hadn't spoken a word, so he couldn't do it then, Did anybody bully ya?, and Zo got all stiff and wooden, Was it someone here?, and everybody started to avert their gaze, the smarter ones also began to get out, as you don't know what could happen, If I hear, it'll be the end of those rotten cocksuckers, if I hear, and Zo shook his head, as if he wanted to dissuade him and let him know that he was alright and that nobody would dare, so there was no need for threats. Then he calmed down a bit, let go of the boy and ordered a rakia, You sing in that gourd, what are you waitin' for?, and that one, all shrunken and limp, sang on, Ooon the local landfill, at which he reached for his pocket and took out a thick bundle of deutsche marks, Here you are, take it, offering it to Zo, who shook his head hesitantly, Here you are, take it, give it to your mother, but the boy refused, and he reached for the other pocket and took another such bundle out of it, Take the dinars, take this, take, and the little one couldn't help taking it, Take it when I say!, and then he turned around and drew the gun, the musician didn't dare to stop, and he wasn't sure if it was advisable to carry on, and he glanced from one face to another, sometimes you can see hatred in someone, which, fortunately, isn't always the case, but that was it, I saw it there from my place, it seemed that the others didn't notice, that they were horrified, there was no sign of the mute one, he'd wriggled himself free, slipped away and disappeared with a bundle of notes, What are you doin', he spoke to them, what are you doin', goddam you, while the people are dyin' all 'round. I went outside and saw the little one kneeling and putting the money away under the linden tree in front of the inn. Then he rose and fled headlong into the dark.

I think that Zo loved the village patron saint's day, in late August, because pinball machines would be brought then, every year I saw him standing next to them, even when there was no-one around, patiently waiting for players, he could even spend an hour waiting for someone to insert a coin and start the machine, and he never had any money to play a game himself, but this seemed not to be the most important thing for him, as was the way the ball came alive and started to plunge down into the labyrinth of the slanted playing field. There was also a bumper car ride, table football, video games, a house of horror, toffee apples, there were also tents with folk singers, halva, silk candies, plastic toys, a lottery, barbecue, girls showing off their tits, a merry-go-round with images of African animals, fathers in white shirts, a punch ball, which recorded the strength of village youths, and there was also a carousel with a purple elephant, a small green horse, a yellow cow, a pink goat and some other creatures. The engine was turning the persistent circular structure, along the upper rim of which scenes from Andersen's fairy tales spun, and this remained so even after ten o'clock in the evening, when the youngest kids would disperse, their mothers taking them home while their fathers stayed to busy themselves with gambling, other men's wives and bloodthirsty fights, the carousel turned around, as if it didn't depend at all on the number of those who wanted to take a ride, but it had its own weird, inexorable logic and will. I can't remember very well the beginning of that storm, a commotion broke out with people running away into side roads, there are no worse storms than those in August, high heels were snapping in a run, children were weeping and disappointed drunks were whining, the funfair staff were skillfully covering their selection of machines, forever ready and accustomed to the most unpleasant misfortunes and bad luck. I was standing on the church steps, being the only one this idea had occurred to, to take shelter there from the rain and the strong wind which was gathering momentum more and more savagely and mercilessly, sweeping everything in its wake, and I stood thus until the thunder moved away and went who knows where, after the storm, to rumble arm wail over other places and other people. It didn't last long, but man never returns once he has left, this is what I've learned and memorized, and the sellers of village entertainment also knew this, but it was their duty to maintain little multicolored lights and cotton candy machines in working order, to persist with as many devotees as the night allows them, and not to get angry, and not to blaspheme, not to curse and not to complain about the trouble constantly befalling them. It ceased and I went down the steps, toward the pinball-machine and table-football room, and Zo was still standing, he wasn't afraid of anything, like the boy from the story, Zo believed and waited for the ball to start rolling, when he appeared, he seemed to be tired, old and exhausted, defeated, as if he'd given up, aimlessly wandering, looking for nothing and nobody, when he spotted the boy lost in thoughts. He came up to him, and I too approached as far as I could without being noticed, I don't know myself why I did this, it was none of my business after all, and he lifted his right arm and put it down on the kid's hair, stroking it long. Wanna play, huh? Come and play, I'll take you a coin. Zo didn't move, nobody moved, as there was nobody else, I was there, and I heard him say: Come on, I've never bought you anything. Play one game, you've never played before, I know you'd love to. Zo stood motionless. That's 'cause you're embarrassed, right? Is it 'cause you don't know how to play? When the rain's over, there lingers the smell from the top of each blade of grass and each stalk and each leaf and each flower, even the concrete releases its own, until then unnoticed smell. Is it 'cause you know nothing? Is that the reason? The man from the bumper car floor began to speak and informed the invisible drivers to insert their coins, press the gas pedal and start driving, warning the others to stand clear of the floor. He clasped his hand and took him along, together they came to the unmoving carousel and stopped, I was close by, I could hear: Come here, you don't have to know anything here, and he seized him with those big hands of his and put him down on the pony's back, a big boy of fifteen, Come here, you've never been here, it moves by itself, you don't have to do anything, and the boy stared, clutching at the metal mane. Then there was nothing and the nothing lasted, the big boy on the ill-suited motionless horse, and a burly, strong man standing beside him. Then the nothing ceased. Nothing, and the man who puts his face down onto his wide open palms, this lasts for a few seconds, then he straightens up and looks at the boy. I'll go and fetch a coin, don't worry, I'll be back, stay there, one ride for you.

Nothing, and the carousel standing still, as if it were made of lead so nothing could set it in motion, colorful things and neon in the night after rain.

SUMMERTIME

We cannot burn the oceans. Despite sparks from the horizon. I walk along the shore for days on end, ruminating about this. I picture myself as a bullet in the belly of the sea. Snows, which is absurd, I imagine snows and black kids in them, black kids' songs are heard in avalanches.

*

This is about epiphanies: they spring from my stomach. I get weary, the body I find myself in is too heavy. I take frequent breaks and divide ideas with a stick in the sand. My mornings are hungry, my wife is gone, she said something, I have forgotten what (or I didn't get it), however, I wouldn't say she didn't know what she was doing. I will ring her at Christmas and sing her something. If not her, my son will certainly want to hear me. He is young and stupid and impressionable, may he be blessed as long as he is like this.

It's been six months since that happened, I left for work, the stock market had collapsed in silence and I gave up. My wife abandoned me, I did everything else. I yearned for an excuse and it arrived when I least expected it. Such are God's ways, and his messages.

At the travel agency I requested a seat on a half-empty plane for an African country. The women working there told me a poignant story about *the dead season*, the story which shortly fluttered away from their hands and I gathered that the two of them had successfully de-masked the general cruelty of the global economy, so I added a word or two about emulsifiers from the pseudo-natural blackberry juice they'd offered me, saying all that was carcinogenic, like *the season* they were talking about, that travels were cancer in color, and that we all would return from them sick to death, but I knew this, I accepted reality and I wouldn't sue the agency when I returned, if the agency existed then. I even said I didn't want to come back. Just in case, I left the keys to my apartment with one of them, explaining to her that there was no one there, that she could wait for me if she wished, that she could freely get married before that, and sell the apartment if it was necessary to deal a lethal blow to the cancer of recession with money. Should my wife drop by, shoot without warning, this was the last thing I said.

As the plane landed, my ear bled. In order to avoid thinking about the pain, I occupied myself with the physiognomies of the other passengers, which disconcerted me. The less time man spends with other people, the better for him.

At the airport in a place called Monastir, I delivered a little performance: I took off my shirt and I kept beating my chest vigorously with my fists. I shouted: *Hello Africa! Tell me how you're doin'!*, and *Hello Motherland! Tell me how you're doin'!* The performance wasn't welcomed wholeheartedly, as is often the case with products of the avant-garde, so I was apprehended by the airport police and spent the following hours in the company of a guy who insisted that he earned his crust at football stadiums across well-to-do Belgium. It took so long for them to believe him, a haggard Arab brandished some sheets, which purportedly said that so-and-so ran over so-and-so somewhere in Germany, so now he wasn't welcome in their democratic country. They regarded me with suspicion, and I openly attempted to interpret the essence of my artistic blunder, which was supposed to contribute to the promotion of pan-African unity.

Then everyone got fed up, the Arab let out a furious moan, gesticulating with his finger that we piss off, all of us, and all of them, and all people at large. The heat was oppressive and I commiserated with him. Standing aside was a black man in gaudy dresses, adorned with primitive jewelry, he twisted in a trance, rolling his eyes and pointing derisively toward the airport door. That witch doctor, he it was that hypnotized us, what he was uttering I heard as *come in, get out, come in, get out, come in, get out*, I wouldn't say I was mistaken, for everything was the same as anything else and for this reason I stepped forward bravely, disheveled and intent on putting away my luggage, all that I had, in a dark cave and forget it for good.

The hotel was an ornate fortress dazed by aromatic fumes of divine gardens, I recalled the yelling cries from the brochures, *Before you, here stayed Wilde, Bowles...*, and all seemed to me to be rotting away and that it was easy to get lost in everything. A wonderful trap, this is how it looked to me.

At first I acted as a voyeur. Hidden on the balcony, I feasted my eyes, brimming with naked bodies in the hotel swimming pool. It was boiling, in that lake of chlorine, and I was writing my long poem *Purgatory*. When I finished it, I signed it as *Hieronymus Bosch, of sound mind, and pure heart.* For a little heap of night minutes I was euphoric. I fell asleep proud and woke up inspired, I rang someone from the room below and read the excerpt on epiphanies. Thrilled and spirited, I swayed from joyfulness, and the woman who answered had a cattish voice. She didn't endure long enough, her dream swallowed the text, and I looked for this woman over the following days, at the crack of dawn, without success.

Rousseau, I have always known, delighted in the benefits of immense luxury. That's why I woke up before the sun and took strolls at the water's edge. Casual walks along the world's membrane entail indifference and absence of practical interests. Rousseau and I are a couple of apostles of lethargy. In fact, I am merely a little buffoon.

At night, the sea spews up tons of rubbish through which I determinedly push my way later on. The rubbish waits to be sucked anew into the quivering azure. The case is the same with me. I wish to overcome the horror of living with myself.

One morning I chanced upon a ruin of apocalyptic dimensions, a deceased hotel. A complex of benumbed, white buildings, where distorted shadows loomed. I approached the wall encompassing the ruin and listened. The ghosts were enraged, my presence distracted them, I existed and disturbed them. I strived to reconstruct, to compensate for what was no longer remembered, to rethink and assemble all that suffocated uproar, incessant movement, people with smooth bodies, words of welcome, falsified poignancy of leave-taking, carnival feverishness, travelers who pounce voraciously on their eleven days (ten nights), and all of a sudden I felt nauseous. I looked back and surrendered myself to the feeling of the freedom of adventure. I felt relieved. I thought of my wife. Out of the wet sand emerged a seagull. It buried its beak into a dried jellyfish.

*

Spend a couple of days in the Sahara, don't miss the opportunity of sleeping in the desert, repeated the agency representative. She was sitting in the lobby, blissfully waving the unrefusable offer. *Did you by any chance plan…*, and I replied that I did have some plans, which were *thwarted*, I insisted on this word. *Thwarted*. And she kept nodding her head, acknowledging the nothingness. I accepted, and I didn't explain to her how come one could accept everything, I accepted because I didn't think I had anything else to refuse, since any refusal entailed an attitude, and I refused to have an attitude, which was still refusal, but… Eventually, I consented to sleep in the desert. I even paid for this pleasure.

We rode in large, white jeeps, I was left alone (since everything was odd and *leap*), the others heaved a sigh of relief when they realized I was isolated and thwarted in every sense. I didn't complain, I had a vehicle all to myself, the driver's name was Memi and he reminded me of the king Hussein. He spoke French, unlike me. Or rather, he spoke, and I didn't, which I found relaxing, all that Babylonian nonsense. He looked happy, entrenched in the language of detestable colonizers. He sobbed and wailed, turning up the radio at the surge of his favorite melodies. We covered hundreds of kilometers, I lay in the back seats, only now and then glancing through the window. Somehow I explained to him my desire to lag behind our caravan, and that he could take a break wherever he wished. It was midday when he pulled over in front of an inn in an unusually stinky seaside village. There was a trail of decay from the open sea, turned partially into a plantation of horrendous black shells. The narrow belt of the seashore between the highway and the sea was an open stretch of land, an exhibition space, where various European artists presented themselves, predominantly modern sculptors. Their monstrous works rotted away in the African heat, burning and sizzling nastily. I went down to those grotesque monsters, passed through a wood of metal freaks, the legacy of pretentious lack of talent. The ground vibrated from the interior boom and I was frightened. Of all those gigantic monsters, ugly beasts, signs of other people's torn souls. I jumped into the jeep hastily, not looking back. I was cold. Memi had returned, babbling tirelessly. Before we moved on, he took a photo out of somewhere in which he was embraced by a woman and two girls. I thought a long, hollow thought.

We didn't see: the Colosseum, Berbers, roadside inn toilets, camels prowling about the stunted vegetation, stage sets left behind after *The Star Wars*, we saw nothing, I decided so, and we reached the Desert Gate first. It was behind an oasis. We got there in time to dream.

The hotel was a mirage, it was clear to me, Memi got inside the heart of the mirage, exchanged a word or two with the phantom of the man at the reception, and went on along an open corridor, like a dancer in paved no-man's-land. We were to sleep there, in front of the Desert Gate, Memi said the others would ride away on their camels toward the sunset, after which they would return richer for a miraculous and beneficial experience, eat well and retire to their cozy little rooms, happy from exhaustion and exhausted from happiness. And no one would know anything about tiny, distraught rodents, haughty and vile scorpions, about existence in livid desert nights and about the disappearance of all traces before daybreak, the Sahara burying under itself all traces of one-day histories.

On the door of my room was a gaping zero. I might not have shut it, I don't know, I went into the cramped bathroom, took off my clothes and squatted down, opening one of the hotel little shampoos, the hot water from weak desert springs boiling down my back. I might have stayed there for hours, before I slumped on the too-short bed and doubled up. I don't know. The air conditioner howled above my head, inside which frantic chimeras raised hell. Perhaps I desired painfully to think other people's thoughts. I don't know. Tireless travelers and their wives cuddling and chirping. This was outdoors.

*

I waited for the night to come to sneak out. This is how I do it. I pushed my way through the hubbub and smiles, sun lotions, fragrant, tempting cocktails, swimsuit straps on round hips. They didn't want their dreams, those vultures of pleasure, they wanted never to cease, such as they were that night. I paused in front of an ice-cream freezer, barefoot and hungry. A flock of stray sirens were stretching in the swimming pool. A young man lost in thought handed me an ice-cream, and I asked him if he had a son, and when he said yes, I replied that the money was for him, that cute little boy. He was confused, and I vanished, lighting a new cigarette enthusiastically. There was no music. They probably didn't want to desecrate the dead silence of the desert. I sat down on the pool edge, dipping my legs into the water and my heart into the whirl of the velvety accents of thousands of human kingdoms. I wished Memi was there, I would have asked him if in that photograph with his wife and the two little girls was everything he lived.

I watched a gracious silhouette immersed in the water. She was edging closer lazily, noiselessly. Some were leaving, to wait for the day. The silhouette's contours kept stretching from the silent strength. A glass fell and broke. No one paid heed. Then she emerged, heavy lividness spilling out of her eyes. I hoped that she would be startled. That she would be excited because I was there, so close. Because I was not afraid. I hoped I would exist for a little heap of her minutes. The slow Russian heaved her breasts, it was thirsty and sticky, words kept shattering and melting down her neck as her chin slightly quivered. I put my hand out towards her, looking about for anyone who could also see her, but I instinctively plunged into blurred contours. And I didn't understand her, the vowels stretching over millions of r's, I leaned my fingertips onto the silver tiles. She didn't want to leave, which was enough for me, the staying there, the acceptance, no matter what, I could no longer lie under the evil barking of the air conditioner, it was tearing me apart, time with too much of oneself in time, this phantom haunted me, the cackle of death older than death.

I took her hand and rose to pull her out of the water into the dark, the rare lights plummeting down toward the hotel room windows. And when I first touched her, I touched nothing, it was easy, transparent, warmth on the palms, the body's fumes under the small, black swimsuit. I lowered my head to look at her, everything between the painted toenails and slightly slanted eyes groaned and strained, bursting, and I wondered what one would do with all that. She left, I followed her because there was nothing else I could do, it was late and everything condensed, without any difference of choice and without any thought of what was not. Nothing remained and this was all that remained.

She kept bending, picking up glasses and ashtrays from the stranded tables, took a forgotten lighter, brought it close to her face, hesitating, wanting to swallow the flame, to suck it into herself while I was there, and then she changed her mind and leaned back onto a discarded lounger. I stood still, I couldn't go any further, thinking about the breath of a lonely man with a saxophone, I wanted to tell her about paradoxes of music, insane theories of the re-composition of essences that were worth hoping for, I am not sure if I also talked about my wife and son, I wanted to, I really did, I would have knocked myself down like an aging and decaying trunk, if I only could, I would shout about that now, how much I wanted. If only I could. If only.

And she lit her cigarette, puckering up her face, circling her hand rhythmically below the navel, closing her eyes carelessly, soaked to the skin, gleaming under the distant desert stars. I wondered whether she did the same for others, whether she was such for others too, who are you?, that is what I wanted to ask her, where did you come from?, why?, I wanted all this, I cared, I seemed to know what to do with the answers, but certainly I wouldn't understand, I would pack her words, carry them with me, something had to be carried, the past, the cross, one had to arrive with something. And there was also a monotonous tone there, an incessant thread of sound, not around us, she couldn't hear it, if she could, then everything was filthy witchcraft and no one had anything to themselves, and I lay on that tone, abandoning myself, I found it easy to do so, I delighted in being powerless, letting others make decisions, I stuck my nails into this sound and floated, floated…

Then she called me, saying nothing, and I knew she was calling me, and yet I looked around, unselfish and ready for defeat, I took off my shirt and lay beside her, anticipating the end of the world. I felt so many things passing through the embrace, and I knew there was nothing behind. I felt a gush out of this woman, and the desert not far away from us swelling, lava burning dunes from inside, images kept returning into the pre-natural chaos, into the original freedom of joyful omni-belongingness. I didn't dare to look at her, I couldn't bear it, no one could, she kept whispering, repeating some words in ecstasy, I knew I mustn't forget, I couldn't forget, because in that case I would have nothing to remember.

She drew my face towards her stomach, and I doubled up and trembled, my hair full of her fingers, my face and lips scratched all over, I wanted to explain to her, to tell her about duration, about time, and she kept twitching, wriggling and panting. Suddenly this all faded away, as in the frightening moon mountains. She pushed me away and rose, and there was something majestic, luxuriant in that. And as she undressed, it hurt. Then it especially hurt.

There, before the Desert Gate. As she stood with her neon shoulders. That flash, sharp, the slit face of the night. I didn't want to ask anything else. Not even why. Not even that. I wanted nothing else. Light. Happy. And as she was leaving, how much life elapsed as she was leaving! And as she regarded me, for the last time, before the Desert Gate. And after that. And now. And always. And after all.

*

I told him to pull over. I got out. It was just after noon. I took off my hat and started to burn. I got worried. I told him to leave. He didn't listen. I told him once again. He too wanted to get out. He thought of his wife and children and gave up. Around us was the expanse of the seabed, which had died. Reddish salt. We arrived in hell. Cracked platform of reddish salt. No man had ever set foot there. I knelt down and glanced at the sun. He put his hand out to me and started to weep. My heavy head bumped into the scorching ground.

*

We cannot burn the oceans. Despite sparks from the horizon. I walk along the dead sea for days on end, ruminating about this. I picture myself as a worm in the eye socket of the desert. Snows, which is absurd, I imagine snows and black kids in them, black kids' songs are heard in avalanches.

GOLEM

Emet.

Ladies and gentleman, highly esteemed lovers of the written word,

A man is jumping off the Charles Bridge. His pockets are packed with truth. Can such a man surface? What imperatives of this world can you execute with pockets full of truth? Truth, it's a burden, the writing of truth, it's a transfusion, it slows you down, death is at your heels, my dear. Who dare, I'm asking you, who dare write the truth? He pauses and doesn't turn around, he knows very well what is behind him, he can hear the approach, the susurration and rustle of silk robes strewn with dark hoar frost. But, is he afraid, the falling man? Since, as we have seen, he's falling off a bridge, pulled down by what he knows about all of us. He loses his balance, exactly that, he loses his footing, because everything has been betrayed, abused and squandered. This is the truth: knowledge about misery. Writing, it's a paradox of proud humility. He who writes the truth bows his head before the heavens, dignified before truth-readers. Pavel Cherny, he's the one we've given an award to, we've given him credit, as he was the only one who was brave enough not to baulk at our atrocity and shame. Pavel Cherny, to my left, isn't an artist. He did away with vanity long ago. He's told me, Great Cherny, that he's merely a witness. He's dismissed style as a forger's mask, he loathes any kind of rhetoric. What is inspiration but vanity above vanities! This book isn't a book. It is. Read The Life of Vladimir, it's the confession of a crime, after which there's no longer freedom. The only thing that matters is Cherny's free fall, accelerated by tons of truth. Try to read this book which isn't a book, take Cherny by the skirt of his coat, try, don't let him fall for you, you won't succeed. Hurl yourself after the drowning man into the Vltava, lunge forward after the herald of the flood, listen to Vladimir and eventually light a candle with your restless fingers. Truth is a grotesque creature. Cherny's merit is this cage, nicely bound, from which there is no escape. Rivers flow, my young ladies with elated eyes. Rivers flow toward chasms, which break their spines. That's the truth.

*

I've been brought in front of the cathedral. This didn't happen accidentally. A spectacle of phantoms. Hanging above my head. Twisting. Their large stone tongues flicking out. It's foggy, but I know them well. I'm old. They cannot deceive me. Giving awards to the dead is hypocritical. Fake redemption. Let it be him, they reach an agreement. Just in case. They dread making a mistake, thinking they are the only residents of the histories of literature. They'll be made fun of, they think. Vanity stinks. Saint Vitus will heal them. All those clowns, obsessed and epileptic. The award is a requiem for my life achievement. My life achievement is Vladimir's non-achievement. Is this a panegyric to him, an ode? The cathedral walls are covered in darkness, as if the day hadn't dawned a few hours ago. It seemed to me that someone was groaning inside. What an exertion of generations of lunatics, what a need to establish a chaotic disorder, an urge to add to the written, to the drawn, an impulse to change infinitely, what a hunger for inhuman proportionality! I don't understand. I'm going to die. Groaning, it can be heard better now, out of the cathedral bowels. All around muffled clattering, they've invited people. I've seen on television. Some who I know nothing about were talking about me. What right did they have to do that? I lived with Vladimir. Now they are all around, the invited. I didn't want them. Ever. Why don't you leave me alone, I'll tell the first journalist. Peace. That's it. I cannot be peaceful next to so many bodies around. I start to panic. It's normal, I'm that old. It isn't proper to live that long. It isn't natural. To live. The scene is eerie, that, the abruptness of the towers jutting out of this world. Where did they think they would get to, those who built them? Babylon, the ship of fools. As if this city were lacking in guilt.

*

I always come to the same place. Those damned trams. It's on purpose, no doubt. We're all being reminded. A thousand years... A thousand years of futile effort. How many of us have attempted to solve... the question of all questions. That voice on the tram, Josefov Station, this is what I loathe. As if they were squeaking, there, around me. I never look back to see who sits behind me, if they stood up exactly at that station. This would be too much. Indeed, we have succeeded, at least here, we have reduced them to a reasonable measure, but still... Sly, that's what it's like! I'm not bound to endure this! How many anonymous letters have I sent to all possible daily newspapers, television editorial staff, political parties aware of the danger! There's no more obvious act of civic courage. To no avail. I know they are here. No matter how few of them there are. Hundreds of them is too many. I know what they are calling for and hoping for. They are suspicious, shrewd. I cannot deceive them. They've read the irony. They're informed, connected, a bunch of conspirators. They've always been like that. Even as they crucified, they connived with each other under the cross. I know they want me, even now, they hope for me, waiting to clasp iron around my ankles. What they set up is traps. They dig holes, like moles, boring, making tunnels. Their civilization is the history of dishonor and hypocrisy. They come, listen to me talk about Vladimir, some of them have always been around. They spy, waiting for a wrong step. They hunt a living man! Fortunately, I haven't been naïve, I haven't given myself away. Some truths die in talent, others are born. I've weighed out well. I've kept a low profile. I've invoked Vladimir in order to hide behind his back. That was a man... I've brought him back to life in order to survive. I've been frantically using him to defend myself for fifty-two years. We'll stay until the end, he and I. Divine justice, I'd say. Some of them happen to have approached me, tapping me on the shoulder and looking me in the eyes. I dream about this even today. I've weathered this, like a man, on my feet. I go to their cemetery in winter. I select a tombstone and stop. I rejoice, but I don't show it. There was a photograph once, they published it: Pavel Cherny pays tribute to all the victims of the pogrom. It was accompanied by a text: In the silence of the mythical crypt of the Jewish people, our greatest writer, author of the brilliant Life of Vladimir, bowed to the shades of the deceased, with no media pomp or noise. At the end of his life journey himself, this grandiose artist, who has built himself into the foundations of the historical truth of the holocaust, finds the time for those to whom he has dedicated his opus. It's them who did this, I know. They took a photo, in secret. They know how much that is... They know. But they cannot deal with me easily. I will never surrender. To them. Those tough reptiles. I observe them every day. The hundreds of them. The remaining ones. This is a nice city. It will push them out, I know. Spit them out. A thousand years was bound to pass. They're here, like on a desert island, with their six monstrous synagogues and the cemetery. And their insane stories. Mordechai, Maharal, Simon and Ephraim, rustling and clinking with those perverted names of theirs. They threaten us! The alive, those who roam their distorted, narrow roads, clutch their bent daggers, waiting. They hope to manure the ground with dust and ashes of the buried. One above another, that's how they did it, one above another. Beasts... The children won't allow it. I've heard of this. Tomorrow is an anniversary and they're going to march. All those brave, young people. Proud people, above all. Cheerful. Free. That's what they're going to do, they're going to celebrate our freedom. The municipal authorities have allowed them, I didn't have any doubts, they are apish cowards, they know it's impossible to halt the lava of our sons' turbulent blood. Who has the right to deny them freedom? The freedom of expression is guaranteed by this country's Constitution! And there's no Europe that can... We'll win, they're also aware of this, as they squat in the exotic museum of the extinct race, with bent knives in their hands... Those mean murderers of ancient and eternal Palestine... I won't live to see, but there won't be, there won't be a station by the name of Josefov, the city will swallow its own excrement. And that... ghetto, it's the foundation on which a magnificent House of Truth will be erected. I can see our children enjoying themselves inside its bright walls, next to blazing fireplaces, intoxicated with the aroma of hot, strong tea in crystal nights. I see, I foretell. Let it be so.

*

There's something unbearable here. As if a surplus of something. The place might not endure so many centuries in a second. All those kings, their statues, sinister specters, have never died. Strangled, poisoned, perfidiously murdered, they are still present. And this is not be borne by man, to be a hostage to all those ideas, beliefs, traditions, by crossing bridges to go from Jesuits to communists, to crash into numerous domes, symbols, languages of strangers who tear the city's past into pieces and take it to their lairs. What is left to man is to vomit, his entrails become agitated from so much presence. Everything is dead, damn it! It can't be here, it must have been buried, all of this! Those who lived before us were lazy as hell to dig, so now we tread over carrions, we humbly speak of this city as being an unheard-of wonder, they believed us, here they come in their hordes and we will never get rid of them. We dig the little that was decently interred, in order to exhibit and sell that, too. Instead of keeping silent! Instead of being ashamed! History is a shame, whoever its owner. We are a shame. An honest man says nothing, he is reserved, he doesn't comment on his past. There's nothing good in the past, this I claim! We cannot restrain ourselves. We brandish bones all around. Kafka, Smetana, Hašek... all those Jews. Havel. I know them. They brought no good to us. They showed us in a wrong light, which we have accepted. The mask they stitched on our faces. And now we are less than a mere prejudice. They've deprived us of our identity. We've consented to be nothing but a commodity. We have nothing of ourselves inside ourselves. Nothing has remained. I had to camouflage, it's life that is in question. And what about the others? I'm ashamed. I'm ashamed on behalf of all the others, if this helps. There's ethics, which is unquestionable. I'm his guardian, they'll come to realize, one day. I've written a book. I'll take it to my lawyer. He'll deliver it to the children who are marching tomorrow. Only then will they understand who I was and why I had to do it this way. Why I created him. When I am gone. My voice will be left behind as a legacy. The words I've written. The truth will stay behind. Someone has to announce it! There's hope, nonetheless. As long as there are the likes of me and those who remember the golden age. We won't be exterminated by those insidious bastards.

I took a walk home and it seems to be quiet. Although I am sure they keep their eyes on me. They lurk around. I've got a long stick, in case they try to push me into the river. Insolent scoundrels. As I was unlocking the door, a neighbor addressed me. He took me to one side, discreetly. He's his country's proper son, he's done a lot for it engaging in secret police jobs. He informed me unobtrusively about a visit by a certain young man, who'd arrived with the first dusk, and who'd been standing eagerly in front of the house. The neighbor offered help to the stranger, who replied that he had a message for me to the effect that I had to show up at the cathedral the following morning. At ten o'clock. The neighbor, being very considerate and quick-witted, asked about the name of the author of the message, at which the unknown one smiled and told him he was an old friend. From younger days.

*

I got up early. Before seven. Order and discipline, I've never deviated from them. That's why I am alive. I turned on the radio. I remembered three pieces of news. That on this day sixty-nine years ago…, and that today certain organizations are marking this historical moment by a Gandhian march. That our Pavel Cherny was presented with an award for life achievement yesterday and that we thus paid tribute to the conscience, not only of the nation, but of entire free Europe. That today, on the tenth of November 2007, bad weather, a windstorm and persistent precipitation are expected. I got up resentful; the thought of the joker who visited me yesterday didn't leave me alone. I decided to go to the cathedral, not wanting to be called sclerotic and senile one day. I must have arranged something and then forgotten. I won't let them make a fool of me. Raise a hue and cry. I'll leave an impression of a man who remembers everything.

I called a taxi and took a book, at random. If he stands me up, the charlatan, I'd better look like a person who's come on purpose and with an aim. They love me. I am the father of the national ethics. They must regard me in awe, the haggard figure of a wise old man devoted to literature and spiritual refreshment. Even though hardly anything can be seen in the cathedral on a day like this. I hope not to catch an illness there, amid the cold stone. There was no-one at the square in front of the cathedral. However, the houses around the square must have been teeming with their people. They are arranged. They are on assignment. They keep track of who I meet. They peek from behind the curtains. There was no-one in the cathedral. And the weather is nasty. Deadly. A torrent that's got in the way between man and God. On a day like this, man does things inconceivable to God, comfortable and certain that God cannot see him. To be fair, I was punctual. I cannot allow myself to be late: being late is not worthy of man. I walked through both aisles with the book in my hand, and noticed a lame shadow disappear behind a low door in the wall. I started toward that place, and then decided to go outside. I thought that the stranger was waiting for me there. I went around the cathedral: grafted harpies bathed in the shower. I didn't find anybody in front and I moved inside. I decided to wait for half an hour, out of decency. I sat down in a pew and opened the book. I wanted to finally discover its title. Immediately it went dark all of a sudden, and I couldn't find the exit. I rose, holding on to the objects I couldn't see. Shortly I stumbled. And fell. I clutched the book all the while. Someone was breathing, next to my face. I didn't dare to speak. I thought the light would certainly appear, so I waited patiently. Then something touched me on the face. It wasn't a hand. Bones and a glove made of translucent skin pulled over them. It scratched. I breathed more and more rapidly and irregularly. You've arrived, it was heard.

A dying woman, I thought. One of those madwomen who kneel for days on end before the icons of Mother of God, I consoled myself. Welcome, she hissed, He's been waiting for you. If only you knew how long he's been waiting for you... I trembled. With the coldness of the stone slabs on which I was lying and with chill. I glimpsed a flicker of a candle passing by the opposite wall and lighting up a painting on which Christ is being interred. And then it was gone. I shut my eyes. The hand was caressing me.

Pavel Cherny! I've heard that voice somewhere before. Sometime. It was indefinable, due to the space and the fact that no-one was there. And due to the darkness. I kept my eyes closed. Nothing would have changed even if I had opened them. Nothing. Pavel Cherny! Do you know who I am? Can you remember? And I thought about how we sent them away. He was shutting the doors on the cars, the trains would be departing as he repeated how much he would love to see what was there. He thought there would be an opportunity for us to go away and enjoy all those places. He would hug me long at the station. He would tell me I was his friend. His brother. He would thank me for having helped him realize. He assured me that he would always be by my side. Until the end of life. I needn't be afraid of anything. He kissed me. Sobbing. Singing in broken German. It was poignant. I've promised you, Pavel. Do you remember? I promised I'd always be by your side. This is what I've done, Pavel, I've kept my promise, haven't I? Admit it, Pavel. And it always seemed to me it could be heard. If you paid a little attention. Despite the clatter of the locomotive and the fluting voice announcing the departure of the express train for Oświęcim from the first platform. We listened to them pressing against one another. Pushing. We were together, Pavel. Do you know? Together. You've disavowed me. How much we've lived through together! You and I. What road we've covered! You've spat on everything. I know what you're going to say. That you had to. Don't try to justify yourself, Pavel. We studied German. He didn't do well. He would become mad. We would go to Josefov then. He kept silent. Pressing his lips together. It was obvious that he was troubled. By all that. He was hopeful. I had a soft spot for him. I knew he could do a lot because he believed. I loved him. You've betrayed us, Pavel. You'd given us up. You've disavowed us. Do you remember, Pavel, all the things you've given up? We were sitting in the station, talking to this officer. We were listing. Correcting each other. Yes, sir, they are Jews, we know them from school. He always knew more than me. Addresses, relatives, friends. He was systematic. He kept a record. You can count on us, sir. You don't have more honest allies than us. Pavel and me. Why, Pavel? Why? One night we went to the cemetery. He was skilful. Deft. Even lovely. He jumped over the fence and held out his hand to me. As soon as he stepped in, he started to demolish. We laughed out loud. They can do us no harm, Pavel. This is all ours. Yours, Pavel. It's here, can you believe it? It's finally here. We overturned the tombstones, euphorically. Are you happy, Pavel? Tell me how happy you are. They'll vanish. Vanish. They'll leave us alone. Forever. You've written that repulsive book. You've written a book of lies. You've given up. You're a liar, Pavel. You're their friend. You've been lying all the time. You keep doing this, Pavel. You're lying! You're lying now! You were lying then! Do you remember what you told me, there, in front, after the cemetery? Do you remember, Pavel? We were cleaning our boots in front of the Old New Synagogue. They were heavy with clay. He pointed at the cemetery gate. This is what we've done, he said, not shifting his gaze. This will stay forever. No-one can take this from us. I'll write a book, I told him then. Everything will be in it. You and I. From the beginning. The Victors' Book. Those who have succeeded. I'll dedicate it to you. To all you've done. The world will know. They have to know. I swear to you. Here. Remember where we were when I said this. I embraced him. We looked up. Toward the ceiling of the synagogue. That book, Pavel. You wanted to kill me with it. Not with a knife. You kind of realize now. That knife is their knife. They would have done that. It wasn't necessary. But, I was thankful to you then. I didn't want them to do it. We were squatting in the shack. Agitation, voices. We were frightened. I even suggested that we deceive them. No-one would know. We completed all the tasks properly. No-one saw. We had a knife. One knife. He carried it with him. He never parted from it. He was the first to realize how dangerous they were. We had a chance. No-one would ever know. Pride. It killed him. The idea of dignity. He didn't want to be like them. To hide, to lie, to withdraw into basements, to pass himself off as someone else. He didn't comprehend the cycle of historical circumstances. If it had been in our hands, it would have lasted. Bad luck, force of circumstances, financial support by American Jews, this decided the war. And he misunderstood everything. It was an apocalypse for him. He didn't hope for another chance. But he had to believe in it. As I did. He said he loved me excessively, so I'd better kill him. He wanted to watch me doing it. They were approaching. I heard them. It wasn't only us, they were pursuing people. Armed, merciless. A death rattle was heard. Many were killed then, for no reason at all. Without a trial. I knew what I was supposed to do, I had to be very quick. He had to die before they enter. It was the deepest the first time. Soft, my hand got warm inside. I couldn't pull it out straight away. He smiled and held my hand. I will always. Stay. By your side. This is what he whispered. And I was left behind to live. I've outlived my promise to him and haven't cut my veins. When a man with a sporting rifle came into the shack, I squealed. Drop dead. You Nazi bastard. Son of a bitch. I'll be the end of you. Scumbag. You'll never kill anybody again. Meet your death. Bastard. Who knows how many times I plunged my knife into him before the man with the sporting rifle moved me away. I was sobbing, and my tears were from his blood. You wrote I was sick. I was mad. You've been ascribing things to me. You've been issuing statements. You've been doing this for years. For decades. You said it wasn't a book, but a diagnosis. That what we believed in was a psychiatric phenomenon. That there was a cure, you insisted. You lamented. I sympathize with the mothers of the massacred. I have some information about the atrocities. The Nuremberg Tribunal has to work incessantly. You filthy deliverer. You went to Israel. You paid them to translate that shitty tirade. The Wailing Wall. You made it there as well. I'm sick and tired of you. Still, I am the one who gave you life. Not the real me, but someone you called by my name. How many copies of the book have you sold? How many times have you betrayed me in order to live? And each of your appearances, literary evenings, interviews, and you know how many there were, all that charade due to a trifle? Your life, and imaginary Vladimir as its pledge? Cheap logic, don't you think? Yes, Pavel. I loved you, too. More than you can imagine. And I've never disavowed you. And I'll always. Stay. With. You. I'll always. Stay...

I opened my eyes, a few candles were burning. The steps were echoing, fading away, and I thought of the lame shadow and the door in the wall. Sounds of wild commotion were heard from outside. It was thundering and roaring, confusion and police sirens. They weren't allowed to march peacefully, the loyal citizens of this country. I rose. A short-haired young man was running toward me, lifting a metal club up high. With clenched teeth and eyes full of some fierce, genuine passion. I recalled the two of us standing in front of the synagogue. He said I was a Jew, that youth. That I was a Jewish dog and he would be the end of me. I bent my head and read the title of the book I'd been carrying all along. It was The Life of Vladimir.

Met.

ESPIRANDO

The remains interred.
Merrily limp limbs
under the moonlit balcony.
In the background some leaves
black as hair.

Kafka

Granddad was a scumbag. I told him this. We played chess. Actually, we simulated a game. He was incapable of retaining a thought. What he knew were the rules. Too little for anything. In his hand he held a pawn whose head we cut off when we were kids. We bit off its head. He pretended to be thinking. This is what prompted me to tell him, this eternal pretense, a travesty of a real attempt. I looked him in the eyes and told him. Then we looked around. Avoiding each other's gaze. He was dirty. He hadn't swept the floor in months. Untidy. Unkempt. Not at all like a complete man. He only heated the kitchen and the bedroom. The other rooms were freezing cold, like the empty stables with the lingering breath of cattle. I often thought that this house was impossible to demolish, that it was impossible to conquer something so heavy. Tipsy as he was, he put the pawn down on a wrong square. He drew his chair to the table and brought his face close to mine. I hated that disgusting, cheap shaving lotion he bought at the kiosk in front of the co-operative building. And he shaved once a week. That week he uttered: You think I don't know that?

He rose and staggered to the pigsty, carrying a bucket of swill. There was a lingering stink behind him. I never saw him again. Alive.

*

When I was told he'd died, I thought I was in for a banal formality. And then the lawyer made himself heard.

Please, be seated, sir. You know, your granddad was, if I may say so, a queer fish. I saw him only once. He called me on Friday, asking to meet him on Sunday. I tried to explain to him that this was out of the question and that I didn't work on Sundays, but he resolutely rejected any other possibility. He kept saying that he would show me a certificate of the complete presence of mind and that he would enclose it anyway, all this with the intention that his will should not be called into doubt by those heirs who might find themselves betrayed with regard to inheritance. He convinced me, you know, we all sometimes make concessions. You're a young man, you'll come to understand with time. He persistently worked on the text of the will, and then he authorized me to read it over his open coffin. He explicitly insisted on the coffin being open. Now, you know he died of a brain tumor and that it's July, so... As you wish. To me, you know, it seemed quite bizarre and I can't say I completely understood him. But, this is also part of my thankless job. What can you do... So, it starts like this:

"I, scumbag M. S., leave my house with all that it contains, I repeat, with absolutely all that it contains, to my grandson M. V. I set a small condition for him – he needs to spend the first afternoon and night between Sunday and Monday after I kick the bucket alone in the house I leave to him. All the other legal successors, my children and grandchildren, are excluded from inheritance. If any one of them complained about my last will, and if they filed a lawsuit in order to determine the necessary part that lawfully belonged to them, I caution all of them and enclose a calculation of the worth of the entire property. If there were any such, let them be satisfied by selling the land or with the savings I possess. Besides this, let it be clear to all of them that I, scumbag M. S., was collected at the moment of concluding this act, and as a proof I enclose a psychiatric report. Luckily, we won't see each other again. Amen."

There, now you've heard it, too. He authorized me to organize the funeral, to inform only you and to forbid priests to, as he said, "come close to the graveyard" during the burial. He paid me everything in advance. He was an honest man, this granddad of yours.

*

The lawyer drove to the village. Since the morning all kinds of things had been making me weary. I listened to the weather forecast, but all I gathered was that something was being forecast. The lawyer had loud enough speakers. The burdensome grayness of almost everything followed us all along. The day before I had phoned my father. He answered, truly pleased. I told him that his father had died. He asked me how I was and what I'd been up to. I repeated that granddad was dead. He replied that this was nothing new. I told him I was going to go to the village, and that the funeral was on Sunday, at 3 p. m. He told me to say hello to my aunts and not to give any money for the funeral, by any means. And to throw the old jerk to the dogs if he hadn't paid everything in advance. He added: or to the lions, at which he giggled.

A large bare-necked bird strutted around the drought-stricken scorched earth we were passing by. Mother was sending her love to me, it seemed. I hung up. I had nothing to tell her. My father's mother died before I was born. The lawyer was talking about retirement. I dropped a hint that music, most of all art forms, manifests the function of disinterested liking because it's abstract, thus giving neither reasons nor grounds for subsequent interpretations. Beauty would, therefore, be utterly inaccessible, if we accept that it's strictly contained within itself. The lawyer shrewdly remarked: Yes.

He accelerated. And turned up the volume. We were almost there.

At the entrance to the village the lawyer gloomily commented: And now, may God be with us.

*

We parked the car under a protruding knotty tree in front of the house, disproportionate to anything around. Unbridled scum paraded through the yard. The coffin had been taken outside and placed on a bier. One man, with his back to the bier, was leisurely pissing. A comically dressed up rogue, adorned with badges with Tito's image, was slapping a stooped old woman's face behind the outhouse. Agitated, over-fattened pigs were trying to swarm out of the sty, seething and foaming at the mouth. Near the sty I spotted a woman that particularly resembled my father's younger sister. Wrapped in greasy rags, she was baiting a strong, black billy goat, that had strayed onto the moss-overgrown shed roof. A short-legged, frightened cat was dragging itself in her wake. I cast a glance in the lawyer's direction: some stinky stuff was being poured into him from a bottle. He was trying to resist them, hopelessly, all uptight and flustered. I decided to think about monkeys.

The massive, bright green gate was wide open. Grand-dad's admirers could come and go as they wished, without hindrance. There were incomprehensively many of them, those Bruegelian creatures. Rare were those who spoke to me, and their yelping showed that they weren't familiar with who I was and why I was there. A bearward was passing by along the unpaved road. The old bear with gummed-up eyes was disturbed by the commotion, it turned toward the yard, in the middle of which was placed the bier with the deceased, and furiously growled. The priest had arrived, but he was chased away from the threshold by the neighbors, the self-initiated security of the gathering. I looked for the lawyer: he was holding on to the garden fence and loosening his collar, looking feeble and dehydrated. I encouraged him to stick it out just a little bit longer. It was a quarter past two. He promised me that everything would be all right. We're grown-ups, he added.

*

He was frenetically applauded as he dragged himself to the coffin. He put on his glasses and seriously studied the text of the will. It isn't a long text, he might know it by heart, I thought. And perhaps it was easier for him this way than to look at the corpse. He straightened up, paused for a moment, everybody went silent, and only then did he begin. He started with visible aplomb and adopted the pose of a brilliant speaker.

"I, scumbag M. S., (as soon as they heard the word scumbag, they seemed to become completely befuddled and to lose even a semblance of self-control, Scumbag, scumbag, they called out, Long live the scumbag!, a few hats flew up into the air, Three cheers for the scumbag!), leave (the lawyer emphasized this word, as if it had a magical, sedative power, and indeed they calmed down) my house with all that it contains, I repeat, with absolutely all that it contains, to my grandson M. V. (To whom?, Who on earth is he?, the woman that had been struggling with the goat ran up, it might have been my aunt, and she squeezed my neck tightly with her gnarled fingers). I set a small condition for him (For whom?, For whom?, Who is he?) – he needs to spend the first afternoon and night between Sunday and Monday after I kick the bucket alone in the house I leave to him (Hurray, today, it's today!). All the other legal successors, my children and grandchildren, are excluded from inheritance (Whaaaaat?, I got free from her grip and pushed the woman, who fell over the coffin, leaning on it with her hands.) If any one of them complained about my last will...

They didn't hear the final part. Madman! Blockhead! They scuffled and scratched each other. I climbed onto the well. Get out! Out! I didn't expect this to be so easy.

They grouped together and dispersed. No-one even glanced at me. I paid the lawyer, who sniveled on my shoulder as we parted. I informed those at the front of the procession that the new burial service was scheduled for Monday, three o'clock. Granddad's face was a livid stain. I closed the coffin and pushed the bier into the shed.

*

I lay on granddad's bed, wondering if he died in it. There was no-one around who could tell me anything about it, I even wasn't sure whether that woman was my aunt or not. I hadn't been here for years, things had changed, and people had changed. I took off my shirt and lay, naked to the waist. No room was darker than this one; opposite the bed was a window, impractically turned toward the neighbor's wall, the kitchen, adjacent to the room, had no windows, and as for the bedroom and hall doors, I didn't open them. The same old chessboard was on the shelf under the switched off television. Some things hadn't changed at all. On the right, diagonally from the bed, was a table that seated eight people. They used to sit there, once upon a time, I've never forgotten this.

Around six o'clock it became horribly stuffy, something was descending to the room from the ceiling and the walls painted with provincial patterns, most often with vegetation ornaments or figures of angels, something like a thick, viscous mass. The doorsteps were lacquered and painted earth brown. Granddad always said he was going to lie down a bit, just to snatch forty winks or straighten his back, after which he would sleep through the entire afternoon. He snored and wheezed in his sleep, I was afraid of this, it seemed like he was experiencing some squeezing and stabbing sensations, leaving him breathless. I didn't think too much about how, by lying in his house, I was fulfilling his testamentary wish, I was exhausted and I'd had enough of all this. I locked both the gate and the front door before I went to bed, so I wouldn't be disturbed. I was sleepy, I remembered grandparents' wedding picture above the large double bed in the bedroom, our predecessors took care of those pictures, pathetically retouching them, making people more beautiful. I closed my eyes and listened to a melancholic trumpet on the radio.

*

It was him, no doubt.

Once upon a time there was a man who had a son and two daughters.

I couldn't make out anything, someone had shut all the wooden window shutters, or it was very late.

He also had a wife, but she didn't live long. She didn't live long, ha-ha-ha-ha...

How did you get out? I shut you in, how did you get out?

He wasn't satisfied with his wife and children, that man, he didn't like them. He wasn't fond of them at all.

Where are you? Where are you speaking from? That something from the ceiling and the walls didn't let me move.

He was unhappy, and didn't know what to do with them.

He was sitting at the table. It was him and it wasn't him, both more and less of him at the same time. He bent over the table, trying to place the chess pieces in the dark. He was confused by the position of the black square in the corner, it was always thus. Where does it go, left or right? Indeed it was him, a yellowish blend of his odious physiognomy was swaying on one of the chairs.

How did you get out? Who let you?

His wife became miserable too, so she began to talk about her misfortune all across the village, where she found some to console her. They were from all parts of the village, and they simply competed over who would console her better. She was also consoled by certain women, but after a while they stopped and left it to men, thinking that they did this better and with more success than women.

He spoke clearly, but it was neither his voice nor his tone. A rasping sound was heard from the yellowish shape. The contractions caused panic and sweating, it didn't look like a dream, I wanted to go and wash my face, or take a shower, to do something with myself.

The man sat so, hoping that everything would be over, but it wasn't, what followed were headaches, fever and insomnia, and the dissatisfaction grew deeper and stronger, and eventually it turned into nausea. The man wondered why such nausea should befall him of all people, and how to get rid of such nausea, since he didn't find it easier even as he shaved, faced with his own countenance in the mirror. His children appeared to him to be monsters that chased him and that would one night sneak into his bed, where they would finally suck the last drop of his blood. He didn't comprehend them at all, he heard them babbling and bleating, so he himself started to address them in the same fashion. As the time passed, it was more and more obvious to him that the children couldn't be his, that he had been deceived and that somehow he had to retaliate for the machinations that he'd been subjected to. It was the most difficult by night, his wife pursued him all over the bed, and he dodged and resisted, he didn't even let her touch him, suspicious of evil spells and satanic intentions.

The bedroom door opened and the darkness from there merged with the darkness in the room I lay in. I could hear someone pacing, coming from one darkness to another.

The man went around the village, doing his chores and listening to voices, which grew in number, multiplied, and with them the nausea. One evening a creature he'd never seen before nor afterward in the village crossed his path, whispered something in his ear and vanished. The man stayed awake that night, chain-smoking by the well, until the dawn. At daybreak he repaired to a man who could solve anything without much ado and entanglement, and ordered ten sacks of cement and ten sacks of sand.

The woman from the picture stood between the bed and the table, approaching neither of them. In a white blouse, she smelled of fog. Granddad didn't turn around. He was massaging his temples, more and more intensely. My mouth was open, I contorted it, fearing that my teeth would fall out from the pressure in the oral cavity.

It hurts... as before. And the man... those sacks... What on earth happened then, I cannot for the life of me remember.

The silhouette of the woman was getting more and more pronounced, pushing his yellowness into the background, her contours sharpened, as if she were carved into the dark space. Light was radiating from her. Something like a train arriving at a station was thumping in my ears, whimpering, groaning and intensifying.

His children asked... and he answered... he answered that they had nothing to ask about, he was going to ask them, where they were when their mother was dying, what they were doing, why they didn't help her, what on earth to ask now? Hmmmmmmm, I'm going to kill my head, to kill, to kill, to have done with it...

Children's faces emerged, one from behind the stove, another on the kitchen's doorstep, the third under the bed on which I lay. Two girls and a boy. I couldn't look, I could die, if there were right moments to die, perhaps I could die then.

Didn't I nicely ask you what we were supposed to do? What did you tell me? Nothing. As you do now. Don't look at me! Step back, I don't want you. Live your life, I don't forbid you. You're safe and sound, stay out of this, it's up to her and me. She herself started it all, go and ask her, stop staring around like you've shat your pants, both you and she are giving me a headache. When I asked what to do, what did you say? Your mother died, what shall we do, you two were constantly sniveling, disgusting kids, you've always been disgusting, disgusting, disgusting kids, I've never been able to put up with you, stay away from me! You, how old were you, twelve? Oh, how you didn't know anything at twelve, I asked you too, if the two girls were as thick as two short planks then as now, you were only whimpering, you kept repeating you killed her, you killed her, I saw it, so what? What bunch of things I have seen! You'll never see what I've seen and heard, you lousy louse, didn't I tell you, say it!, didn't I tell you, so say it then, damn you, you perfidious bastard, and what did you do, what did you do, you did nothing, didn't I ask all of you, didn't I ask each one of you what do you think and what do you think and what do you think, and you all thought what I said was the smartest thing, and when I told you, perhaps you'll have to go to a children's home, perhaps to relatives' homes, perhaps out on the street to beg, blabber all around what shouldn't be known, what happened then, nothing happened then, I'll tell you, you stood as you're standing now and you were silent as you are now, and you pulled the sacks too, all of you did that, in twos, a boy and a girl, a girl and a boy, twenty times so, that's why I was constantly saying, don't get close to the well, there's nothing interesting there, and oh my god what I listened to out of that well afterward, there's neither day nor night, I didn't fall asleep for twenty years after that, there's nothing in the well, and you tore a sack on the threshold so I had to clean up until the morning, so they wouldn't see the cement, how did I know who could come by and what they could ask, rotten halfwits will ask all kind of things when it's neither the time nor place for it, mother had left, did you get it, you and you and you, I explained it clearly, and it was so, she had left you, I didn't, here I am with you now, she'd gone, a devil had come for her, it wasn't me who drowned her, you bonehead, you said you'd seen, a devil it was, and anyone could be a devil, you and I and she and she and the children of yours, and the one I left my house to, let him see what all of you were like when the devil came and you didn't utter a word and were silent instead, as if he would pass you by if you stayed mute, you ragged fools, you're grown up but you're good for nothing, good for nothing, the devil was here, he left and passed, no, he didn't pass, he stayed, who knows where, in the well, under the sand and cement, that woman was heavy, stiff as she was, I struggled with her, where was the devil then to help me, this is what I'm asking you, why didn't he come up to me to whisper in my ear as he'd done the previous night, and how come he left you with me to suffer even now, heavy burden, heavy burden, what did I live to see, and what I didn't live to see, stay away from me, you freaks, I'll throw the Bible at you believe me don't go round me damn your sick seed I have things to do even without you, you're standing there motionless give me a hand let's throw some more sacks more sackssacks letitgo whenIsay don't hold it tight shewasalso holdingtightmay godsave hercrazyhead leaveityouwon't meI'myourfatherfather I'mtellingyouleave it lealealealealealealealealealealea-lealealealealeaaleaaaaaaaaaaaaaaaaaaaaaaaa

*

It ceased. The clock struck three after midnight. The bedroom door was neatly shut. I went out into the yard and moved away from the house. Accidentally I leaned against the well. The bier with the coffin with my dead granddad was in the shed. I've seen the dead who didn't fully die and the living who died but went on living. When the day breaks, I'll go and search for that one who can solve everything without much ado and entanglement, and I'll order two cans of petrol.

THE TALE OF HOW I. I. SETTLED THE QUARREL WITH I. N.

Krapp the Listener's New Life

Soundtrack: Earth – The Rakehell

I wished to be left alone, I felt the need to add and subtract, to perform these operations. I felt I could no longer bear it, I packed and left, they didn't make any trouble. They seemed not to care, one left, another came, as elsewhere. Still, I'd performed plenty of good jobs and done a few serious favors where expected, one would think they would miss me more. I was getting slow and, which is much worse, I was becoming indifferent and slack, and this could prove fatal to the job; perhaps no one else noticed this, but I did, and it was enough.

Rare are those who prepare and leave in peace, traditionally everybody finds it embarrassing, on so many occasions I had seen people leaving the Firm stooped, confused, as if nothing else awaited them. Work wasn't my life. I don't know what was, but work wasn't. I set off on the longest holiday ever, with the intention of never returning to the town. No one noticed my absence, the nature of my job didn't leave too many friendships, I had done with my family years before and those idiots neither called nor contacted me. They probably thought that somewhere someone had beaten me all over and buried me, I wouldn't be the first or the last. They failed to take into account some important little details: I am not stupid, I love myself for inexplicable reasons, and the Firm takes care of its former employees and collaborators, It doesn't want anything unpredictable to befall them, It attempts to spare them certain encounters and conversations.

About fifteen years before leaving, I had invested part of my savings and bought a weekend cottage on a half-wild estate close to the river. I warmed to it the moment I set my eyes on it, the infrastructure wasn't entirely completed, the owners of the other buildings were people from the towns in which I almost never set foot, so the possibility of recognition was reduced to the theoretical minimum, and after September utter quietude would prevail. Then I could get benumbed to atrophy (or hibernation), to let go of any unnecessary vital functions and think about everything, if I felt like thinking about everything. The weekend cottages were far enough from one another, I'd chosen an altogether average prefabricated little house, comfortable and well isolated, sequestered among tall trees, barely visible from the road. About eight hundred meters further away was the river, on its banks there were stores, a pharmacy and pubs, some of which were open even out of season, which made life in the relative wilderness perfectly agreeable.

I rented out the town flat, with the tenants' obligation to pay the annual rent in advance, we arranged this with my lawyer, the procedure took thirty minutes or so, they were quiet people, a married couple with two little children, those who look forward to everything as if they were at the beginning of who knows what. I informed them that the lawyer was the one who they would consult in the event of any repairs or misunderstandings with the neighbors, I gave them all the furniture as a present, and wished them all the best in their later life and work. I sounded correct, openhearted and well-intentioned. I got to my new permanent place of residence by car and after a short stocktaking of the situation on the spot I decided to leave the car, with a symbolic compensation, to the owner of a small store which sold fishing equipment. I stopped at this store anyway at least once a week, the guy wasn't difficult or chatty, apparently aware of the troubles that words could bring about in man's life.

I arrived at the beginning of April, furnished the cottage, made it habitable, adapted it to the current needs and patiently embarked on the project of automation and routine-making: I got up before seven, did the morning gymnastics, took strolls to the shore, bought three packs of cigarettes and daily press, the cigarettes lasted for twenty-four hours, and I didn't bother with the press, putting it aside unread, this aspect of simulation was necessary, because man becomes suspicious the moment he gives up the practice of the insane majority. I'd seen enough of such cases, and it made me want to throw up. I've always refrained from alcohol, because it makes a jerk of a man. While shopping, I uttered courteous remarks of a meteorological nature, so I didn't get into the trouble of discussing daily political questions and sport results. True, the sales clerks didn't bother much with my personality and work, shortly they learned by heart the list of foodstuffs I bought, so even the tiniest semblance of our mutual communication was missing. I had a high-quality fridge with a freezer, I washed, dried and ironed the laundry on my own, and I never bought a television, the source of universal retardation.

I can say that the summer was the most unpleasant season for living in the out-of-civilization circumstances, due to the organized mass arrival of tourists from towns whom I couldn't avoid. Still, by the tactical reduction of movement I managed to prevent them from disturbing my painfully acquired harmony: I reduced the number of times I went fishing, I bought a carton of cigarettes in one go, mentioning the summer heats as an excuse, and I even managed to sleep through a larger portion of the day, thanks to the tablets the local pharmacist issued to me. As soon as I arrived, I told her a nice lie about my past, she believed it entirely, which was strategically important for me, I took a large number of medications and a cream for hemorrhoids, and I didn't feel like going to the nearest larger place. I became most obviously close with this girl, she was dullish and unaware of anything, she constantly bothered me with the story of a world different from the one in which she lived, and this was utterly irritating, but she had a full and pleasant voice to which I wasn't immune, despite the years spent in the world's dump with all-around smart-asses.

Thus, the autumn was setting in, I mostly spent time fishing, lying, I didn't have a single book because of the notorious fact that books are utter bullshit, I kept scratching myself and forgetting, and this act of forgetting was the priority of all priorities; the world will forget you easily, but how can you forget the world? I spent pleasant evenings on the small balcony, swinging in a comfortable chair and stopping the flow of any thoughts, even those apparently innocent and harmless. This is how a representative of the Firm found me, while I was breathing in the forest resin, in a chair in front of the cottage, a step away from a new dream.

They always look the same, one could say that I myself looked so to the others. People you can neither recognize nor remember, such people are what the Firm needs. He tried it cordially. Good evening. It isn't good. Why not? How are you? The same as you, with the difference that I don't steal. They didn't tell me you were like this. What did they tell you? We'll talk about that later, take it slow. How are you? None of your business. You won't offer me anything? No, cut it short. How are you getting on with the neighbors? As always. I don't know them. Do they know you? Ask them. You know why they're sending me? No, but I can see they've sent you. You have two men near here. I have no one. OK, don't go too far with that. They are here, three hundred meters further down. They're older. Older than you. The season of hunting the retired ones? Everything else is all right, the mummies have now left? You're tiring me, the boss sends his regards. You know what it means? Let me hear. The house is bugged. It isn't like yours, prefab, it's real. Mine is also real. Theirs isn't prefab, fuck it. They're staying here for five more days, as far as we know. I've brought you a computer. What for? To listen to the recordings. Why don't you come over to fetch them when it's over? I'll come if there's anything. You'll call me. Why would I do that? Because the boss sends his regards. And because you never leave anything unfinished. And because you are by chance closest to them. Have done with that, and then you can keep on dying in peace. What if there's nothing? Nothing.

The next day I went on a tour of the surroundings. What did I come across? God save me from enemies of the state and dissidents, utter dumbbells and fanatics with complexes. Two senile old men who wrap themselves in expensive sweaters as soon as the sun starts going down. One of them had already reached the phase of jaw atrophy, he couldn't open it and release the passage for a little spoon of vitamin syrup, the other tucked his hand into a plastic bowl full of menthol sweets and left it there. Liberals, that's what was said. Those who wish to alter the face of the society radically. Anti-state elements. They always end up like this, when they don't end sooner, with whole-hearted assistance. A writer and a retired university professor, a common combination, charisma and its servant authority. Those who exert themselves in their youth out of naïve stupidity, later they overplay it, they get to like taking a little from the other side as well. They are caught in perversities, whores do for them on frequent travels, paranoia, obsession with total control and transfers of power. It's easiest with such people, an intelligent and resourceful photographer is their demon. They never take care, because they are convinced of the absolute morality allegedly innate to their enlightened being. At the slightest hint of blackmail they become horribly low and servile, they start offering what is not even requested, shrinking from the public to whom they'd presented themselves falsely and who they'd educated on infantile premises. The Firm loves them and never abandons them. Dementia makes them even more valuable, in terms of experimental exoticism. These two had become the target of interest because, according to all operative findings, they hadn't communicated with each other for decades. All significant factors of liberal milieu have tackled this affair, studies and feuilletons have been written about it. The left wing was considered decapitated due to their quarrel, had they successfully settled the conflict, it was thought, the social reality would suffer from drastically fewer imperfections than is the case today. The Firm wanted to fathom the essence of their belated encounter and figure out what such an encounter could mean.

I let five days pass. The information of their leaving was certainly valid, so on the sixth day I entered the empty house effortlessly and collected the equipment. It was only inside the house, the resplendent, luxuriously furnished building, that I felt quiet resignation because of what I was doing. The boss's greetings weren't threateningly intoned, they had nothing to threaten me with, it was an appeal to the conscience of a good and obedient soldier who responds unquestioningly to any, even the most incoherent command by the headquarters. They flattered the old man's vanity, setting me the task and letting me prove to be still an efficient executor. Man is a miserable, stubborn dog. A miserable dog. A piece of shit.

I decided to start before going to sleep, hoping there would be some things on the recordings that would cheer me up and alleviate my uneasiness caused by the unwillingly accepted task. I set the laptop on the night stand and turned up the volume.

Transcript 1: 18 IX

I woke up puzzled. It rarely happens that I fall asleep immediately, I stayed awake for a long while, but I didn't recall a single uttered word. I warmed some water for tea and replayed the recording. When the water boiled, I put a tea bag into a mug. Eight minutes passed, I keep the black-tea bag that long in the water. There was nothing. Sounds, in irregular intervals: the shifting of chairs, flushing the toilet, the faucet, coughing, loud yawning, steps. Nothing else. I checked every ten minutes. The same. Nothing. I spent the day listening to their day. Nothing at all. Only in the late afternoon did I catch something of a human voice. From the recording I concluded it was ten past ten in the evening. At first I couldn't make out what was being uttered. I listened dozens of times. Good night. Good night. Only this.

My first reaction was the feeling of utter nonsense, but it shortly changed to the benefit of a rare sort of the mean satisfaction of a man who returns deceit for deceit: it would be marvelous to deliver five such recordings to them with a plea to send lots of greetings to the boss. I took an interest in the reason why they would meet after so many years, if they weren't on speaking terms. I decided to listen to the next recording in bed, too.

Transcript 2: 19 IX

Ivan. Are you asleep? No. We could have raised a revolution, Ivan. You think so? I'm sure. We could have. We could have.

I was fascinated. A series of short utterances, some time before dawn at that, I slept through them, only when I woke up did I manage to find them, hidden on the recording. I continued with the nightly listening technique.

Transcript 3: 20 IX

How do you look on that, after all? You think we did everything that was in our power? I think we did. I wonder more and more often how the future will look upon us. We are the history that has written itself. It seems important to you, what we used to say? Yes, it was important at the time when we talked and wrote. We are history. The world wouldn't be the same without us. The world wouldn't be the same without anyone. You're right, but without us it wouldn't be, what can you know about a world without yourself? We are the ones. Understand? It's strange that you wonder about that. We had roles. Those were good roles, carefully written, masterfully performed. Yes. We've been alive for a long time, Ivan. Long time, Ivan. You're tired of it? I don't know. I've read Sartre, again. Me? I don't know. I read sheer words, not the meanings. I love to observe the letters, this fills me with joy. Then it's all right, isn't it? If it fills you with joy? I don't know. Imagine someone was listening to us now, what would they think? I don't know. Why would anyone listen to the two of us? There are so many others. But, we are history. We are. That's why. Were you afraid in prison? I don't know. It was good there. I wanted prison. I believed in the usefulness of experience. Prison is good. Do you believe in anything today? I don't know, Ivan.

I really don't. We used to lie quite a lot. I don't know if we can trust anyone, or anything. You live only if you lie. We wanted to live, you and me. Who knows, they will write about this sometime. Who knows what they will be like, whether they will know how to lie better than us. Those lies of ours, they weren't for nothing. Do you remember how it all started? No. And you? No. You'd dare to remember if it was possible? I don't know. It's all the same now. I cannot get frightened. I wear dentures and I've grown accustomed to them. After this it isn't bad. And the illness? Yes. We've been alive for a long time, too long. How was it for you to live? As if I lived. As if I actually lived. As if that was really me.

I couldn't wait for it to finish. The way they talked was anguished as befits the old age, the words and sentences being a few hours removed from one another, they made me sick, man shouldn't look like that. The despair was all too tangible, I didn't want them next to me, but they managed to tear away from the recording and occupy my space and time. I was in two minds about the last couple of recordings, but the disciplined instincts set me back to the listening position.

Transcript 4: 21 IX

Dentures are an obligation, you know? It's like having a child, you have to take good care and never lose sight of them. Never at all. You had children, Ivan? You know I did. I don't know. I've forgotten. Do you remember them, your kids? Remember at least how many there were? Two. Are they alive? Only this matters, if they aren't alive they cannot harm you. That's what I think of children. That's why I never had any. Now I sleep peacefully. You, Ivan, you don't sleep peacefully. I'm sorry for you. You always have bad dreams, you say all kinds of things in your sleep. If I talked in my sleep, you couldn't understand anything. That's because of the dentures. Shall we eat fish today? Fish is healthy. We should follow the advice. Today's press is brimming with advice. In the past you had to search for it, and today you have to approach it hermeneutically. Which advice is your advice, it isn't easy to define. I agree. Remember when we had a mutual woman? Heeheeheeheeheeheehee, we were pioneers. Not even in Amsterdam was it so easy then. We had a really nice flat. We should have stayed there. Nothing stopped us from shutting the door and not allowing anyone in. We had a woman. What else did we need? I sometimes think we were ungrateful, Ivan. We justified our ingratitude with the reasons of evolutionary nature. The constant of dissatisfaction won't improve the world. If we had that woman now, huh, Ivan? We could… dictate to her. She would keep silent and write, smiling once in a while. What did we want? I can't remember what we wanted… How did it finish, with that woman? She left. The bed was huge, we slept in it together. You slept next to the wall, she hugged you, I hugged her. You two criticized me for turning on the other side during the night. Sub-consciousness proverbially betrays you. Freud is the father of the pseudo-scientific slip. We talked about who we would rather meet, if we could. I said: Freud. You said: Ashurbanipal. She said: "I'd like to get to know myself." Today I barely know who I am. You think she got married, that woman? Or she found it enough to be in the twofold marriage with us? It was a marriage, Ivan. A genuine community. Who are you, Ivan? Who are you? Bad breath is the worst. The dentist tells you everything's all right, but the bad breath doesn't disappear. You make enquiries, but no one wants to know about your bad breath. Or they know, but don't want to know. Or they know, but they find it strange why you haven't enquired about it. Bad breath is evil. It perches in the diaphragm, waiting. Then you stop noticing it. The less you yourself notice it, the more clearly the others smell it. This is the irony of bad breath. I missed you. I couldn't talk with anyone like this. You were my husband's wife, we know each other well. How many decades have elapsed? I don't know. I care about matter and substance. Society isn't what interests me. The law of society is the non-observance of the norm you try to establish. That's why society is illegitimate. I can imagine an angel. I couldn't do that in the past. I don't know. Let's say, I could go away once more. To see Easter Island and die. I hope I can expect that much. My children went away once. Never to return, but they write. They often write, they both have nice handwritings. Those are old-fashioned letters, unlike these electronic ones. The handwriting is always the same, but I know they both write them. Socialist education had its shortcomings, but it was genetically healthy. Ideologies have their own genetics, too. They must be old, my kids, if they're alive. I don't know. The letters keep coming. Who knows who writes them. We are here until tomorrow. Yes. It's passed quickly. You wish you hadn't come here? I don't know. No. Did you invite me, or did I invite you? I don't know. It's nice here. You've got a nice house. Isn't this your house? Aaah, yes. Probably I invited you. I don't know.

I don't know. You think we'll see each other after this? I don't know. No.

I was falling into lethargy. I wasn't ready. My energies were burning off, only limpness remained.

Transcript 5: 22 IX

Komodo dragon! I've got it! Komodo dragon! Ivan, Komodo dragon, I've been talking to you about it all the while! That's its name, Ivan, where are you? Ivan? Oh dear… Oh dear, dear, dear… How did that happen to you? You're weak, that's what it is. You even bumped your head, that's what it is. What shall we do now? Does it hurt? No. Not much. Don't move. I'm here. First I need to lift you and rest you against the bed. Then you'll drink some tea. We'll see later what to do and how, we have the whole day before us. And it's better that you fell now than tomorrow. If you fell tomorrow, we wouldn't leave. You and I are old travelers, Ivan. Wait, I'll think about which side is the best to approach you from. You were talking about a dragon. Yes, will you listen to it while I'm lifting you? Yes. It, this dragon, can live up to thirty years. You think it's not much? I don't know. It's two meters long, approximately like the two of us. It's the biggest reptile alive, the biggest, you've heard of this? No. I don't know. *Varanus komodoensis*. It's like the two of us. However, it cannot live long. Thirty years only. I think it's still not much for those that are two meters long. Again, some people think that all stories about dragons originate from Komodo Island. As far as I'm concerned, it might be so, but maybe it isn't. All stories originate somewhere. Peter Owens, you've heard of him, Ivan? No.

He invented Komodo dragons. Don't they exist? They exist, but he invented them, get it? One wouldn't say you don't get that much. You used to understand everything. This man Owens had his own zoo, somewhere in Canada, he deported the dragons there. A dragon zoo, that was the name. Not Owens's, but of the zoo. May a zoo be named after the two of us. At Two Ivans', that's a good name. I want to rise. That's my boy. You've always been strong. Willpower. The komodo zoo was somewhere in Mauritania. You said Canada. Yes. All the same. Sorry. I'll take you under the armpit and lift you. The Komodo dragon is a mammal. Most often it dies of bacteremia. Bac-te-re-mia. What are its enemies? The wild boar, raccoon dogs and bison. You're heavy, I'll try to lift you again. There, mmmmmmmmmmm, oops. Fine? Fine. I say it's fine. Bravooooo! There, relax. The female lays eggs. You said it is a mammal. I didn't. It can overpower a man the size of a boar. If a man dies, the Komodo dragon will eat him. This is the sad side to the story. It bears kinship to a tree trunk. Instincts, climbing, relative safety. That's it. You're lost in thoughts? Yes. What are you thinking about? About suitcases. We should pack. We have the entire day before us. We no longer have it. You think that much time has passed? I don't know. Yes. You look nice when you're thoughtful, enlightened. You've always been like that. I used to keep front pages with your photographs. I still keep them, although I don't know where. I don't know where. Did we have a thermos? I think so. And a hot-water bottle? We didn't. Why didn't we bring one?... You're cold? No. We don't have the entire day. We have the bus tickets. We had them validated at the station when we arrived. And here, how did we get here? There was a taxi. There used to be a taxi. It has three numbers, that service, the first is nine. We'll recall the others. We have some time left. I don't know how good it would be for you to rise from there. I'll bring you lunch down there, have lunch and then you'll rise. I won't. I want to rise. Good. You want to rise. It must have started like this. What started? The quarrel. What quarrel? Our quarrel. We had a quarrel, remember. A small, intimate quarrel, which grew into a large, public quarrel. We used a quarreling discourse, both of us. Yes. We did. It must have been important. For the society. Yes. Don't let it disturb you, it's past. It is? It is. It's no longer? The society? It's past? What on earth did the two of us do, how did we do it… No, no, no. The discourse is no longer. Uh-huh. It's nicer that way. For the society. It will tolerate this more easily. The society tolerates even Komodo dragons, despite everything. It isn't a society. What is? Nature. What is it? I don't know. Want to rise? No. Shall I bring you the lunch, down there? No. I told you I'd rise. We've had a hard time today. We used to cope. Cope. We used to. You've taken the medications? No. I'm not ill. You had some medications, I've seen them. Those are vitamins. Yes. Hey, how we used to. We still travel, which is fascinating. Yes. Impressive. I'll miss you, when we get back. I don't know. I will miss you. You've never told me so. I haven't. No. Yes. I will. I've never got used to saccharin. We should have gone to Ecuador or Costa Rica. Imagine, if bananas cost as they do here, how much are they there? Heaven. Does it exist? We had a sledge, in our childhood. There were lots of us. Now only me. We had Christmas tree decorations too, then mother put them in a shoe box and took them to the loft. They were bitten through by mice there. It was no use putting the bitten decorations on the Christmas tree. Man easily gets disappointed. One should never forgive one's parents. Milkshake with a bacon flavor. Unbearable. Bourgeois mindset produces nutritional kitsch. I'll write about this. It is known: you get silver after you lose gold, and bronze you win. Ivan? Yes. Asleep? No. I love you. You know? I've never loved anyone the way I love you. I don't know. Yes. I don't know. You really love me? Yes. Ivan? Yes? This Komodo dragon, it's got wings? Of course. It's got wings. Good night, my dear Ivan I. Good night, my dear Ivan N.

I took my laptop and headed towards the river. I didn't stop, and I reached the bank before daybreak.

LENG TCH'E

All angelic dancers are dead. Maria Schneider is dead. Marlon Brando is dead. All waltzes are therefore crippled. Helno is dead; he sang to the most sorrowful waltz ever. *C'est un bien triste un bien triste sort.* My husband is dead. I watched pigeons nestling against one another, against hospital window panes, tucking their little heads into their soft, puffy bodies. Tarararaararararara, tarararaararararara, tarararaararararara, *C'est un bien triste un bien triste sort.* Helno died, the waltz has remained. My husband has died, I've decided not to brush my teeth nor wash myself ever again. We made love, for a long time, we occupied a huge portion of the night with our bodies, then fell asleep, I dreamt about a carousel, I woke up, it was May at the end of March, sunspots on the walls, my husband did not awake. I cried, dancing naked and alone in front of the mirror, crying, that was half a waltz, not even a tiny one, merely a half, I danced before the mirror and my dead husband as persistent observers. I saw someone in the mirror, but it wasn't me. I might have been somewhere in the background of the mirror, where there was something you crossed over no longer to be here, walking, tirelessly, a direction chosen or not, but you had to choose yourself again for what was beyond there and for anything there was. I recall that my late husband grinned as the late Helno sang.

The man in the funeral parlor asked me if I wanted to have another look at my husband, and the carousel in the dream was turning in the rhythm of a waltz. Carousels never turn in such a manner. The undertaker passed me a pencil timidly, to sign something, and I couldn't remember my name. It wasn't important from that moment. There was a man in the dream too, and the man in the dream had a wooden stool, which was beside the carousel, and the carousel was in a deserted field, and a storm was gathering, but we all knew it was far, so far away, and we were safe, and the man in the dream had a ridiculous beret, tilted to a side, he was grinning facetiously below the moustache, the carousel was turning, and he was playing, he had a small French accordion. All of a sudden, the wind blew the hat off his head, but he kept on laughing, I was the only one on the carousel and I had a light summer dress on, with every color on it, I was holding fast because it was dusk, and it was a poignant dream in which the most important thing to do was to hold fast, the storm-gathering wind was raising fine dust, and I yearned and hoped that there was a painter who would ... all this, who would ... all this, all this...

I didn't wash myself, days went by, I threw away the toothpaste and the brush, both toothbrushes, one day a young man knocked on the door, a mechanic, he was repairing a failure in the building, he kept apologizing and asked me if I had a key to the cellar door, and I told him I had no keys whatsoever, there was no door and I did not live here, I did not live at all, and that I would never descend to any cellar and check what there was under the ground if I were him, no, by no means. Then

I lay down, the sticky, elastic time was stretching like rubber on fire, I kept putting my head down on my late husband's pillow, now that pillow was mine too, I had two pillows and I was at a loss what to do with them, so I shifted between the pillows, in the slowly burning time, I ate nothing most of the time, I drank water now and then, but water could not extinguish the pyre on which time was smoldering. The phone kept ringing, I did not answer, I pretended to be asleep, until one night, someone asked if that was me, I told them to hold the line and got up with great difficulty, I drew near the mirror, looked in the mirror, and said, hello, I don't know if this is me, in the mirror I see a woman with too-long black hair and I don't know who this woman is, I wouldn't say it's me, but then I don't know who else it could be. No, I don't know who you are, I'm certain of that, that's how I finished, I don't know, I don't know, I don't know. The signal of all phones in the world is an *a* and it must have been proposed long ago that this *a* be the basis of the method on which the world is tempered.

After the incident with the night call I switched off the phone and the fuses. There was no longer the menacing buzz and harsh lighting, apart from some remains of light falling inside from the street, but that much I could bear. I tried to eat, with my mouth and eyes open wide, straining, struggling to suck in those mouthfuls, but in most cases something would throw them out, some kind of spring tucked under my throat preventing this, and I struggled, pulling my hair, digging all-too-overgrown nails into my knees and face, slapping myself, taking stale food, contorted on the floor or on the bed, my hands clasped fast around my stomach. I imagined Hunger approaching me, and Hunger looked different every time, greeting me politely, and I would return the greeting convinced I was acting disgracefully and abominably. Then an itch started, unbearable and irritating, and my peacefulness disappeared, a neat everyday life became a terror of itching, I scratched certain spots on the body so much that they started to bleed, causing scabs and bleeding lines to appear, I was proud of them because they testified to my persistence, I rolled all over the floor, the bed, eventually over the tiles in the bathroom as well, and then, defeated, I stepped into the tub and turned on the water, freezing cold, filthy at first from stagnating in dilapidated pipes for several days, and the water flowed and I shivered, crying, and it was a dreadful image, a woman squatting in a tub, crying, it was unnatural, a woman shivering, something had snapped in the order of moves, and I was ashamed of myself like that and of all such individuals in all times in any world. I thought of my dead husband and his last touches, and that was something holy, like a legacy, the fact that I was the last he touched, there, you're no longer alive, I think I uttered this aloud.

Then I started to make calls, during night chases for runaway sleep, most often an automated voice answered, informing about the exact time, it's thirty-one minutes and fourteen seconds past three, and my husband has died, he was thirty-one and his heart stopped, that's what I was told and spared any acerbic terminology, it's thirty-three minutes and fifty seconds past three, Jesus was crucified, thirty-three is, for all that, more than thirty-one. And my husband was my dead husband was my buried husband was my sleeping husband, no one could die in their sleep, he died in his sleep, he didn't die, he merely fell asleep, never to awaken again, an eternal sleep, which was not death, or sleep was death and I could no longer understand anything.

I discerned that the walls were moving, each second of my sleep was abused, heedless, heedless I was, if I could let such a thing happen, walls were all around, bending over me like sinister guards, I had nowhere to go, so I decided to open the door. Hands from everywhere, my mother's, his mother's, his sister's hands, my head passing through those hands and all fingers on those hands passing through my hair, and every single day filled with words and sobs, you should see a doctor, you should go away. The doctor said there was something inside me, that it was healthy and that it would be born if I wanted it, and an anorexic colleague of mine handed me an envelope, lowering her glance, there was plenty of money, some kind of assistance, and a brochure, Easter in Vienna, they'd paid for me, they miss me, they can hardly wait for me to come back, she told me to have a good time and ran down the stairs, and I shouted after her, Easter is never spent in Vienna, but on a cross!

Nevertheless, a few days later I got on the bus, my headphones throbbing with Helno's voice and my womb full of a dead man's semen, we left at midnight, some girls kept looking at themselves in the mirror, the city all around, we drove through the night and I wished to become a night lantern in the west, I wished this metamorphosis, forever a night lantern which no one needed. *C'est un bien triste un bien triste sort*, a smiling girl in the seat next to mine asked me if I loved French music, I replied curtly that I loved waltzes and that I'd had a husband who was now decaying, later she slept for hours on end, and I pretended to sleep for hours on end. Towards daybreak we stopped at a solitary petrol station, I lay down on the cold asphalt, my eyes anchored in the departure of the night.

Everything was a lie, I swiftly noticed, significance, history, culture, monarchy, Europe, international organizations, atomic energy, tourists, Germans, Americans, Italians, opposite this lie stood the attraction of death and its architecture, even the hotel was a tomb, the Pyramid Hotel (... *not a bad choice at all, far from the centre, a large and comfortable four-star hotel, surrounded by a big park, situated opposite the huge shopping mall Shopping City Sud, with a modern congress centre, an indoor swimming pool, a wellness centre and a number of other facilities...*), a terrifying crypt, a false lying lie. I wandered, frantically and headlong, in St. Stephen's Cathedral I was asked for money to climb down to the bottom of catacombs, the same on the underground, there was no difference, under the ground, above the ground, a lie and blind hallucination, the history of deadness, I took a map of Vienna's underworld, as I studied it, walking briskly, I came across Pestsäule, I stopped and said, to the one growing inside me, look, look at the lepers, saints and angels, look at the hundred and fifty thousand corpses, and none is your father, and then chased by unbearable dread I ran across the Vindobona excavations, it was getting dark, a Requiem resounding out of St. Michael's Church, as if the boy Mozart were playing it at his commemoration. The next day I deliberately got lost in the Labyrinth of Schönbrunn, lying low and cooing to the semen inside me, singing quietly, the White Rabbit passed by, looking at his watch in panic, and an officer of the city of Vienna in charge of security in the castle yard threw me out, after lashing me with ugly German words piled in solid German syntactic series. The streets suddenly turned dark, Easter in Vienna, a city with no inhabitants, I roamed alone, Easter in Vienna for Jesus and my dead husband, I stopped in front of a stall with sausages, thrusting myself among several silent pilgrims from thenetherlandsitalyformeryugoslavia, we ate together, they and I, and it was nice in front of the stall, we were chewing in silence, like African cattle in programs about survival.

I went back to the room with some verses on my mind, a Frenchman, not Helno, a troubadour before him, also dead, moving incessantly, a French maniac in fear of standing still, born on the fiftieth birthday of Elizabeth of Austria, this lunatic beatnik world traveler sang of Easter in New York, that was his song, but I found my own in it, as the doctor had found it inside me, and I wrote a poem, Easter in Vienna, I ripped it out of the womb of his poem, sensing the presence of Elizabeth of Austria, the lunatic beatnik world traveler poetess Titania stabbed with a needle file, I sang myhis lines, the melody was a lullaby for the semen living inside me, they complained from the neighboring rooms, I was loud and inconsiderate and I didn't care, Lord, today is the day of your Name, In an old book I read about your passion, about your anguish and your effort, your words so humane, Weep down in the book like sweet gentle rain, And I am in my little room, there on the side, like a creature miserable and voiceless, I'm waiting behind the little door, waiting to call him! Oh, it is You, it is God, it is me – it is the

Eternal, Then I did not know you – as I do not know you now, And I have never prayed to God, not even when I was a child, And yet thinking of You tonight I'm scared, My soul's your doleful mother as painted by Carrière, Widow mother in black at the foot of your Cross, Beyond all hope and tears, mourning, mourning such loss, I am bent and I'm feverish as I stride on down, Carrying my shrunken heart into town, Your split-open side blazes like a great sun, And your hands send sparks flying all round, And yet, Lord, I have braved a perilous voyage, To contemplate the cut beryl that holds your image, May a froth of ferocious despair never appear, I'm sad and I'm sick; perhaps because of you, Or perhaps of some other, Still, certainly because of you, The streets now deserted turn blacker, I sway on the sidewalks like a drunken old slacker, Scary darkness juts out from houses in big flaps, I'm scared, I'm being followed, I daren't even turn my head, Hobbling steps approach with threatening taps, I'm scared, I'm fainting, I stop dead, A hideous weirdo walks by and has me stagger, With a sharp look that cuts and hurts me like a dagger, Lord, nothing's changed since the end of your Reign, Evil uses your Cross as its cane, Lord, the dawn has slipped in cold as a shroud, And has laid the skyscrapers bare in the clouds, Already the city is alive with sound, The trains bound and rumble and shudder away... Trains thunder and roll underground, Bridges are seized by the railway, The city trembles, Cries, smoke and fire, And the raucous wail of steam sirens, Fevered from gold sweats this throng, Jostle and cram down tunnels dim and long, In the maze of plumed roofs the sun's so murky, it's your Face gobs of spit have made dirty, Lord, I return tired and mournful, alone... My room is bare as a tomb... Lord, I'm all alone, I've fever... My bed is cold as a coffin... Lord, I close my eyes, my teeth are chattering... I am too alone, I'm cold, I'm calling you... A hundred thousand spinning tops dance before my eyes... No... a hundred thousand women... No! A hundred thousand cellos...

I stopped and all those gathered in front of my door left, ears pricked, I listened bewildered, breathing in and out evenly, and on the bedside table was a thin little file, and in the armchair opposite me a woman was seated, her face concealed by a brown fan, in a long, black overcoat, with a leather parasol in her free hand. You are dead, I said, and she said, you can be that as well, pointing the parasol towards the bedside table, my husband is dead, I uttered, but she was silent, and I had less and less room in my lungs, condensed air, spheres of flaming air cremated my lungs, why don't you die, she said mildly, Elizabeth Maria Amalia Elizabeth of Austria Sisi Titania the Austrian empress and Hungarian-Croatian queen, where did you come from, I asked, I was at the lake, strolling, she said, Lake Geneva, I don't know what happened to me, I've come to tell you to die safely, she rose, with all bodily energies compressed in her childlike waist, she didn't remove the fan from her face, and she lay beside me, come and die, like me and like all, Sophia and Rudolf, and I was sobbing and saliva was all over my chin, she touched my hand and put the file on the wet covers on which we were lying, here, now you can, and I'll take you back, to the lake, I promise you, we'll go back to the lake and when the time comes I'll help you give birth on the shore, there, next to the water, don't fret, I'll write a poem about your dying, come, I don't know what happened to me, please, I have no one to walk with around the lake, please, I'll sing to you, I'll be good to you, I'll hold your hand and you'll caress my dead children. Sisi too fell asleep in my dream never to awaken again.

All of a sudden, it was no longer day, and there was no longer the file, and there was no longer the faceless empress, there was nothing, I went out, along the corridors of the Pyramid, it was Saturday, people were having dinner in a lavishly illuminated hall, metal kept clicking against ceramic plates, murmur, a constrained tourist ritual. I avoided all this, pausing for a while before the sight and continued through the winding arteries of the barrow, languidly, speaking to the creature inside me, do you want me to want you or do you want me not to want you, the creature remained silent, do you want to die, I entered a room crammed with sportswear-clad men and women, bright and strong men and women, potent, sweating all over, running on unstoppable mechanic treadmills, twisting on grotesque devices, I grew sick of this body torture chamber, I passed through an empty changing room, not turning on the light, echoing between regularly placed lockers containing swimmers' stuff. At the swimming pool it was aggressively intimate, dimmed lights, silence, floating bodies staring somewhere through gigantic shrubbery, old men, lying prostrate on uncomfortable deckchairs, steam from a sauna and a Turkish bath, sporadic flashes, good evening in German, I didn't reply, two tall, thin young men with long penises in the children's pool, splashing each other and cackling at the top of their voices. Oppressively warm, suffocating, I undressed nervously and put my things aside, tucked them together and put them down on the wet floor, remaining in black underwear, that was all I wore, I straightened myself up as far as I could and stepped into the lake of the Pyramid. Then came Nothing, and everything ceased, and thoughts were dying unfinished in my head, unborn thoughts about everything were replaced by images, short, simple images, simple visual records of the surroundings, things and objects, the closest ones, the reachable, a gallery of such images devoid of any crossed perspectives, an idiot's one-dimensional, insignificant, meaningless photographs. I swam back and forth between the pool edges, passing by lazy, walrus-like bodies, diving, it was too shallow, I moved to the pool with a jacuzzi, a billion energetic bubbles battled with my hips, breasts, thighs, my stomach for hours on end.

I stayed alone, lying thus, with hands extended over the edges of the small pool, I reluctantly rose, half past eleven, headed toward the Turkish bath, behind the closed door a curtain of essential oils, pine, eucalyptus, I froze, it started to roar, to howl, out of nowhere, a choir of ghosts, I staggered from fear, my recently deceased husband's stiff smile, I think, Lord, of my unhappy hours, I think, Lord, of my hours before me, I shuddered, singing a song I'd seized for myself, I pushed the door with my shoulder and rushed out. Not far away was the sauna, and I wanted to calm down, only to calm down, an old man was sitting inside, swaying back and forth, back and forth, the old man in a trance did not notice me enter, a naked old man, flabby, yellow and exhausted, drowsy and absent-minded, his withered lips drawn over his false teeth. I sat opposite him, holding onto the small bench with my hands, go to sleep my baby, close your sleepy eyes, the lady moon is watching, it spilled out of me, and I returned it to the one parasitizing inside me, the old man jerked, startled, muttering something in German, staring at me, he rubbed his eyes, yawned, and went on looking. He pointed his finger between my legs, resolutely, and uttered something, a command, I looked in his direction, he said it once again, this time showing understanding, I said, what do you want from me, he said, you have to undress, you have to take off all the clothes, take off your underwear, I cast a glance at him, there is a sign, there, in front, take off your underwear, there are rules. Easter raindrops were plunging onto the glass pool roof. I rose. I'll be a mother. You fascist. I'm a mother.

Midnight by the hotel clock, as I went out. One midnight my husband, an eternally sleeping man, told me about a poem by a Frenchman, a lunatic, beatnik and world traveler written for me, titled *You are More Beautiful than the Sky and the Sea.*

Sunday morning, rain, I stood before the Hundertwasserhaus for several hours, motionless, we'd been waiting, an entire day had been wasted, I was told so, and I went to the Prater. It was deserted, the old, Big wheel halted, its red gondolas hopelessly hanging in mid-air. I mounted the one on the platform, no one was there, and I seated myself. When one was on top of the wheel, one could see the entire city of Vienna. I clutched my stomach tightly with both hands. I think, Lord, of my unhappy hours, I think, Lord, of my hours before me, it was raining in Vienna, the wheel was standing still, I no longer think of You, I no longer think of you, *C'est un bien triste un bien triste sort, C'est un bien triste un bien triste sort.*

HIDDEN/GHOST TRACK:

ABOUT A DOOR

I could write a word or two about that little one, and how he stands before a door. It was Saturday, going on for six, the little one had arrived and stood there, nothing else was happening. I don't know who could find this significant and what might be written about nothing. The little one was nondescript, but such was the time as well, history found itself in a rift, sizzling with all kinds of follies. Many stand before many a door, there is nothing new or special to it, people and doors have been written about: it is not an exceptional topic. I am rather well informed about that kid. Twenty years have elapsed since then, I am not certain, however, that time matters much. Time both passes and does not pass, both exists and does not exist. The same is true of that little one, there, he exists anew, exactly as he used to be, whether it is twenty years or less is all the same. Whether it is he himself makes no difference, since I see what I see. People believe what they want to believe, not that they are desirous of other things beyond measure. They can trust me too, nothing will change if they do, I will recount what I wish. Let them do whatever they want with it. There is paper and there is fire and that is all there is. The little one slept in a big room. The thing with the door happened in spring, which is fair to mention, so as not to look down on the kid with unnecessary pity, because it wasn't cold in the room that morning, but it was gloomy, the boy could still make out: a bed, another bed and yet another one, a table, a wardrobe, a mirror. Noteworthy objects, and their silhouettes. The longer you are in the dark, the better you are at discerning things, which is no trifling advantage. The little one found it hard to get up before five, which he never came to terms with, it would be right to remark that there is something evil and sadistic in the voices you hear at that time, the voices that have to tell you this and that. I wouldn't say that the number of those who would listen at that time is too large, nor is the number of those who would listen at all too large, but there are stories and that is it, nothing can ever change the fact of the story, because there is no interest to it, none whatsoever. No one expects anything from a story, no one wise. Some voices were heard from the dark, which was a usual occurrence, otherwise the little one wouldn't get up, someone had to do that for him, the people from that house are dead today, and probably it is the same with the house, and it is painful to remember all those dead people from the dead house after so many years, perhaps twenty, perhaps less. The rest is a lie, long-term memory distorts, and what remains is not even semblance, it is other than what it used to be, a story that is not important, for if it were important, people wouldn't die, neither would houses die. Since everything is equally significant and insignificant, even the kid before the door is equally a story, whatever opinion one would have of it. It is possible to tell billions of stories about that little one, there were things there, but he himself would opt for a few, if he had to make any choice, because beyond the chosen stories lies calculated sense, and there is hope of the existence of calculated sense, and the hope arouses thought about stories as messages to be deciphered before it's too late, as if anyone would benefit from them. The trouble with the story about the door lies in the fact that nothing happened, and the sooner we all acknowledge this, the sooner we will give up story-telling illusions. The little one stood there, the world also stood, and this lasted a while, an image of this has remained, which is a story, and all this is about that image/story. The story about the door is an apology of any conceivable stasis, if it has to be anything at all. Even today at that very place is the door, the river, the small bridge, the electro-technical school, the high school, the court, the Youth Club, the museum, the access roads, the red kiosks, the bike racks, the whole lot is still there. River, concrete and lawns. Children from the school buildings run along the river, until it turns too cold to run. Some of them run, others look at them calling out remarks, all this around the river is rather intensive. On this particular morning I would write about, no one was there. It was different in winter, prisoners were brought out to clean the snow from the bridge, monitored by guards armed with automatic guns. They reached the town market later on (if I am not mistaken, the market is no longer where it used to be, but I couldn't swear to it) and kept on cleaning, as the village vendors who came to work first insulted them, shouting: "Boo convicts, boo bandits, it serves you right, fiends!" Hard-working folk they are, with a proverbial high opinion of themselves, those vendors working in such a manner. Again, no one thinks the best of the river, although it has no smell that wouldn't be in direct relation to people and their affairs, the crowd, however, passes by and swears at the river with a common aside to the effect that only a couple of other places have a similar odor: the dog pound and the starch factory. So, the little one heard one of those voices, once alive, and he followed it. Old age suffused the adjacent room, he passed through it sullenly, in the bathroom he washed and partially roused, he washed his hands with a bar of yellow children's soap (only this soap was used in that house, until it disappeared [which is good for the principle of association]) and he squeezed the Kolynos toothpaste onto his brush (only this toothpaste was used in that house, until it disappeared [which is also very good]). He rinsed his mouth, returned to the kitchen, sat down and leant on the table, tea with indistinctly sweetish taste was already there, and next to the full mug scrambled eggs were steaming, looking appetizing, but the little one didn't feel like breakfast, he had about ten minutes to do so many things, rushing about exhausted and perturbed in the sense of feasibility and ultimate effect. That's why he did this: he sprinkled half the contents of the saltshaker onto the plate with the scrambled eggs, rose and went back to the dark room where he got dressed in no time, it sometimes so happened that he slept the night in the clothes he'd worn the previous day, but this was not such a night, as the morning was not as any other, at least he always thought there was something extraordinary in that, there, before the door. Behind the door was supposed to be music, and this is what he hoped for when he first arrived in this town, it was supposed to be the town of music, unlike the town in which he was born and raised, where there was no music, there was no such music, there was not enough music, this is why he cherished hopes that he would find music in a new town, but it isn't always easy with hopes. He had arrived and for months now he'd been struggling to convince himself that he was not mistaken, that music was everywhere, that that was the right music, but this wasn't the case, music was elsewhere, in different places and with different people, behind the door some people squirmed, he got to know them, shortly afterward his interest in most of them waned, and a similar fate befell the fake town of music, or the town of fake music. Some sort of music was heard there and music experts ascended the stairs clutching printed notes in their hands, obedient students following in their wake, thinking they would acquire the privileges of music, which was not happening, and there were also those apathetic when it came to music, most often they didn't feel like anything, so they morosely observed the world out of the music cage. Of all disappointments, and their sum total is certainly not small, which a random objective calculation will show, the greatest is disappointment in music, when it occurs, and when it actually occurs, one stays in a noisy, deafened space, which is a paradox, but a true paradox, and against this paradox one can do nothing whatsoever. The little one stood before a mirror, it was unlike later before the door, on the other side of the door there could easily be nothing, whereas with the mirror it was completely different, this is why he liked to stand before the mirror, in winter, in the afternoon, it was dark outside, and in the depth of the mirror it wasn't dark, which delighted and encouraged him. He looked at the clock, it was a solid Soviet clock, a present from a man now dead, the time was approaching, he took the box with his instrument and started on his way. The voices greeted him cordially, their owners were alive at the time, and there seemed to be no surprises to brace oneself for. However, the knowledge of the fake music in the fake town of music was indeed a surprise to get prepared for, but who would know this, so now it was necessary to suffer in the school of music, and such boys never suffer, they resist and think they have all possible rights and that they are isolated from the craved outcomes which they await in secret, in no time at all they turn into revolt per se, raving and confronting the illogical construction they qualify as the system, and they do so in order to pay knightly deference to the object of their own animosity. The little one shut the gate behind him and went on to catch the train, trains have an advantage over people, they are indifferent toward the urges of leaving, coming and arriving, there were not many trains back then, only a few would steal out of the historical rift, and the little one had to wake up before five so as to successfully catch one of the rare trains and get there in time for the Saturday orchestra rehearsal, because, for all the lies about music, he was dedicated to the duty the music suggested, and he didn't want to betray it, as it was gradually betraying him, turning its back on him mercilessly. To be better than music, it was a strong argument when it came to the showdown of self-reconsideration. He comprehended this a month before the event at the door, he kept trying to play a modern French composition, a vibrant solo de concours, he wasn't even close to success, but he sensed he knew what it was supposed to be like, and that on the other side there were those who sounded successful but felt nothing, he was brimming with this intuitive achievement, shut inside a sterile classroom for individual instrumental instruction, upstairs, on the second floor, the left wing of the corridor, he lifted a window shutter and spotted kayakers pushing hard away down the river in their elongated vessels, elegant, powerful and handsome. It was worthwhile sticking it out until the end of March, everything was to change then, and it was possible to avoid the waiting room, up until then it was cold, those who waited smoked, wrapping in newspaper sheets something that wasn't regular tobacco, playing cards, worn Hungarian cards showering across laid pigskin bags. As soon as the first April days came, passengers waited for trains sprawling on the station platform, the boy occupied a place on the corroded railing remains, and out of habit I kept turning my head in the direction of the north, where the railway signal was changed, announcing the arrival of a train. A man's day was born out of hubbub, the boy reasoned, squeezed between workers, villagers, and passengers, overhearing the tongues rattling against the palates and filling-studded cavities, it seemed to him that he was invisible, and the invisibility was good, like the mild sun on the neighboring fields. The rhythm of the train like morphine and like blue-green and like steam from sometime machines used for paving periphery crossroads. The boy tried not to lose his footing as a reflex action, he didn't need to, he couldn't fall, because he didn't have anywhere to fall, people canceled the laws of physics, you couldn't leave and get to a place where there wasn't a human language, because you thought in a human language which was hopeless, but without which you couldn't even be hopeless, you couldn't be anything, I knew that, even then I knew. And there was a piano: a badly tuned piano, a classroom on the ground floor, and there the little one made it his habit to pursue his search for forcefully interrupted dreams, the piano was man's friend, for it sounded without too much invested effort, touch was all that was needed, tone was touch, there was no question there about the quality of tone as aesthetically decisive, the quality of touch, the touch drawn in the eardrum. The kid would do this when he was early, he would enter the classroom, remove the lid from the piano and touch it, nothing else, because you could do nothing else if you wanted your dreams back, the plan would have to look exactly like this. And the train was slow and it was slowing down, the suburbs, tilting hangars, industrial landscapes for accustomed observers, nine kilometers in linguistic secretions, nine kilometers to the fake town of fake music, times nine in return and nine the next day and the day after, perhaps not on Sundays and perhaps not on some other days. I longed for air. The door was opened, the train was in motion, despite the metal warning signs, no one paid heed, Moses was anachronism, those in the front jumped out chased by the mania of urgency, deftly, skillfully, landing on their feet and going on toward hospitals, markets and smoky, distant contours. The little one extricated himself so as not to be seen, even though no one noticed him, who cared, and the little one crept in between the freight wagons, jumping over their couplings by means of safety handles, it smelt of coal and serious poverty. When he crossed over (he duly paused and glanced left and right, although there were no trains at all) I started over the embankment, there were other ways as well, even better ones, but he chose this one, and he stuck to it, since even then the little one's character was unwavering, conservative in decisions he held for a certain reason to be correct, an unfaltering, fanatically and stubbornly consistent type. The absence of people and sounds started right after passing the embankment, I cannot say I noticed it immediately, it could easily be a projection caused by the time distance and the wish to write the effects that were actually missing, but that determine the story structurally (and semantically, inevitably). Still, in the maze of streets down which he had to plunge in order to reach the school, the little one passed the university, a butcher's, he liked to loiter in front of butcher shops and count the pieces of bacon on hooks and piled sausages, he passed by a pub where students of mechanical engineering studied, and by a dark house entwined in ivy, in that house and its damp, depressive yard he would find a student of Italian and her elder sister, he would spend an afternoon with them, they would laugh, he would leave and not forget any of that, this would happen three years after the day I am writing about, I recall it clearly, but I can by no means gather why I recall it, of all the things I could have memorized, why this and what it all means, when you remember it and recount it on. Then, there were the prison walls, it was once known that the prison was where the court was, there was no transport for those with escape on their minds, fustiness, lichen, and countless stories about what went on behind the walls, the little one had an inkling of it, of the solitary confinement cell, of the attic and the basement, the Sunday soup made from prison pigeons, two Hungarian watchmen and an insane colossus of a guard, who insisted on working night shifts, so as to welcome ruffians, rapists and irate alcoholics eagerly, and beat them bloodthirstily without witnesses, investigators and record-keepers. When one stands opposite the court façade, the school seems to be in a luminous depression, surrounded on all sides by buildings taller and more monumental, shadowy and stately: the school looks as if it had sunk into something, slipped into all those melodies buried in its history. Viewed from the bridge this depression is even more pronounced, and the little one wondered whether the real secret, what it was that was painfully difficult to fathom, was in the depths of the river, rather than behind the door of such an insignificant and worthless building. From that very bridge, which is merely a strictly functional steel monster, descend some steps, the little one went that way, and I heard my own steps, it was Saturday, and it was early, and it was the first time I'd heard anything in that noisy, deafened space, on the paved path leading up to the semicircular concourse in front of the door. I walked on leisurely, and a flash of the only just risen sun leant on my shoulders, crisscrossing the cold school façade, as if only then did the little one become wide awake, he raised his head and stopped, at first almost bumping into the door decorated with tall, iron figures. I know no one who has heard the sun, or colors, or smells, or shadows, but I can confirm that all this could be heard then, there, there was nothing else, the little one kept spinning in wonder, searching for the place where all this was coming from, but there was nothing, and in the nothing was heard the sun, and melodic colors, and shadows. The boy took another half-step and touched the door, which usually opened easily, I'd done that so many times, but nothing happened this time, one couldn't go any further, and I stayed there, before the door, alone, many people consider possibilities, this is one of the possibilities, solitude, absolute solitude, it is also a possibility, but as a theory, as a draft or a logical resultant, because there appears perplexity, one wonders: how am I to know who I am if there is no one else, and there was no one else there, someone had locked the door and forgot about it, someone who didn't expect that anyone like me existed. What else could anyone be but a totality of relations, whereas there, before the door, there was no such intimacy, I stood in a membrane that had suppressed the world, swelling with light, not heat, not winter light, but only light, only from the effect which shaped scenes and spaces and without which there was not even that trifling nothing with which I was left before the door. The second time I almost thrust at the door, disconsolate, not because I looked forward to what was behind, but because absolute solitude was equal to absolute deafness, I muttered a chain of meaningful syllables and they didn't find adequate sense, because they were addressed to no one, and they couldn't be addressed to me, because I was nothing, like all that piled stone around, lawns and indifferent trees, syllables and words ceased on the inside of the membrane, bursting, fragmentizing, vanishing. So I stood before the door, I could go back, toward the safe place where I'd come from, to search for trains and their tracks, wherever they led, wagons and embankments, to recall, that above all else, but I didn't recall anything, and then there was nothing, when you could recall nothing and no one, there was no movement and no way back, toward the trains and tracks. The boy standing still, the door standing still, the world standing still, and they in it, the world-membrane which everyone had forgotten and which had forgotten to inhabit itself with concepts, notions and beings, I found myself there, with my instrument, my useless instrument, a whistle that did not announce itself in tone, since tone was duration, vibration in time, and time had canceled itself, annulled itself, for me to stay there all by myself before that door, all on my own, man was seldom less than that. And I cannot say that it lasted, because it didn't last, and it did last, if it hadn't lasted, I couldn't recall it, and I couldn't invent it and write it down, the boy stood, not anticipating anything about the man writing about the boy who didn't know anything about him, but he knew that there was a door through which you couldn't pass, and you were made to stand and wait for another man to write another door, the one through which people and boys passed, covering the same different ways, you waited for a man with the right words, with passwords and codes for people, boys, women, girls, alive as well as the dead, what was, what wasn't, what could have been and what would never, never, never be. The sun behind the back, the river. Paper, fire, and everything there is.

ACKNOWLEDGEMENTS

Some of the stories have been

published separately elsewhere

"Good Night, Captain" in *Offcourse Literary Journal*, Albany, New York, September 2014, Issue 58.

"Leng Tch'e" in *Rock & Sling, a journal of witness*, Spokane, Washington, November 2014, Issue 9.2.

"About a Door" in *Gutter Magazine*, Scotland, February 2015, Issue 12.

"Summertime" in *Word Riot*, April 2015.

"The Tale of How I.I. Settled the Quarrel with I.N." in *Mud Season Review*, Vermont, USA, June 2015.

Girls, be Good

by Bojan Babić

"Girls, be good" is an omnibus novel that consists of twenty short stories connected by a single framing narrative: just after the fall of the Berlin wall, foreign investors feel good about the investment climate in Eastern Europe and decide to open a huge toy factory in ex-Yugoslavia, where they are going to produce a hit range of toys designed for girls: small, plush lemurs called Aya, that will be sold all over the world. Before long, though, their optimism starts to feel out of place - the war in Yugoslavia begins, and the factory, having only produced one edition of the toys, has to shut down production...

The Flying Dutchman

by Anatoly Kudryavitsky

Some time in the 1970s, Konstantin Alpheyev, a well-known Russian musicologist, finds himself in trouble with the KGB, the Russian secret police, after the death of his girlfriend, for which one of their officers may have been responsible. He has to flee from the city and to go into hiding. He rents an old house located on the bank of a big Russian river, and lives there like a recluse observing nature and working on his new book about Wagner. The house, a part of an old barge, undergoes strange metamorphoses rebuilding itself as a medieval schooner, and Alpheyev begins to identify himself with the Flying Dutchman. Meanwhile, the police locate his new whereabouts and put him under surveillance. A chain of strange events in the nearby village makes the police officer contact the KGB, and the latter figure out who the new tenant of the old house actually is.

Nikolai Gumilev's Africa

Gumilev holds a unique position in the history of Russian poetry as a result of his profound involvement with Africa. He extensively wrote both poetry and prose on the culture of the continent in general and on Ethiopia (Abyssinia, as it was called in Gumilev's time) in particular. During his abbreviated lifetime Gumilev made four trips to Northern and Eastern Africa, the most extensive of which was a 1913 expedition to Abyssinia undertaken on assignment from the St. Petersburg Imperial Museum of Anthropology and Ethnography. During that trip Gumilev collected Ethiopian folklore and ethnographic objects, which, upon his return to St. Petersburg, he deposited at the Museum. He and his assistant Nikolai Sverchkov also made more than 200 photographs that offer a unique picture of the African country in the early part of the century.

This volume collects all of Gumilev's poetry and prose written about Africa for the first time as well as a number of the photographs that he and Nikolai Sverchkov took during their trip that give a fascinating view of that part of the world in the early twentieth century.

- Solar Plexus by Rustam Ibragimbekov
- Don't Call me a Victim! by Dina Yafasova
- Poetin (Dutch Edition) by Chris Hutchins
  and Alexander Korobko
- A History of Belarus by Lubov Bazan
- Children's Fashion of the Russian Empire
  by Alexander Vasiliev
- Empire of Corruption - The Russian National Pastime
  by Vladimir Soloviev
- Heroes of the 90s - People and Money. The Modern History
  of Russian Capitalism
- Fifty Highlights from the Russian Literature (Dutch Edition)
  by Maarten Tengbergen
- Bajesvolk (Dutch Edition) by Mikhail Khodorkovsky
- Tsarina Alexandra's Diary (Dutch Edition)
- Myths about Russia by Vladimir Medinskiy
- Boris Yeltsin - The Decade that Shook the World
  by Boris Minaev
- A Man Of Change - A study of the political life
  of Boris Yeltsin
- Sberbank - The Rebirth of Russia's Financial Giant
  by Evgeny Karasyuk
- To Get Ukraine by Oleksandr Shyshko
- Asystole by Oleg Pavlov
- Gnedich by Maria Rybakova
- Marina Tsvetaeva - The Essential Poetry
- Multiple Personalities by Tatyana Shcherbina
- The Investigator by Margarita Khemlin
- The Exile by Zinaida Tulub
- Leo Tolstoy – Flight from paradise by Pavel Basinsky
- Moscow in the 1930 by Natalia Gromova
- Laurus (Dutch edition) by Evgenij Vodolazkin
- Prisoner by Anna Nemzer
- The Crime of Chernobyl - The Nuclear Goulag
  by Wladimir Tchertkoff
- Alpine Ballad by Vasil Bykau
- The Complete Correspondence of Hryhory Skovoroda
- The Tale of Aypi by Ak Welsapar
- Selected Poems by Lydia Grigorieva

- The Fantastic Worlds of Yuri Vynnychuk
- The Garden of Divine Songs and
  Collected Poetry of Hryhory Skovoroda
- Adventures in the Slavic Kitchen:
  A Book of Essays with Recipes
- Seven Signs of the Lion by Michael M. Naydan
- Forefathers' Eve by Adam Mickiewicz
- One-Two by Igor Eliseev
- Girls, be Good by Bojan Babić
- Time of the Octopus by Anatoly Kucherena
- Soghomon Tehlirian Memories -
  The Assassination of Talaat
- The Grand Harmony by Bohdan Ihor Antonych
- The Selected Lyric Poetry Of Maksym Rylsky
- The Shining Light by Galymkair Mutanov
- The Frontier: 28 Contemporary Ukrainian Poets - An Anthology
- Acropolis - The Wawel Plays by Stanisław Wyspiański
- Contours of the City by Attyla Mohylny
- Conversations Before Silence:
  The Selected Poetry of Oles Ilchenko
- Zinnober's Poppets by Elena Chizhova
- The Hemingway Game by Evgeni Grishkovets
- The Secret History of my Sojourn in Russia
  by Jaroslav Hašek
- Mirror Sand - An Anthology of Russian Short Poems
  in English Translation (A Bilingual Edition)
- Maybe We're Leaving by Jan Balaban
- Death of the Snake Catcher by Ak WelsaparRichard Govett
- Hard Times by Ostap Vyshnia
- The Flying Dutchman by Anatoly Kudryavitsky
- Nikolai Gumilev's Africa
- Duel by Borys Antonenko-Davydovych
- Vladimir Lenin - How to Become a Leader
  by Vladlen Loginov

More coming soon…